TO THE BACK OF BEYOND

TO THE BACK

OF BEYOND

Peter Stamm

Translated from the German
by Michael Hofmann

GRANTA

Granta Publications, 12 Addison Avenue, London W11 4QR

First published in Great Britain by Granta Books, 2017
First published in the United States by Other Press, New York, in 2017

With the support of the Swiss Arts Council Pro Helvetia

Originally published in German as *Weit über das Land* in 2016 by
S. Fischer Verlag GmbH, Frankfurt am Main

A CIP catalogue record for this book is available from the British Library.

1 3 5 7 9 10 8 6 4 2

ISBN 978 1 78378 329 8
eISBN 978 1 78378 331 1

Text design by Julie Fry
This book was set in Bembo and Whitney Light by Alpha Design &
Composition of Pittsfield, NH.

Offset by Avon DataSet Ltd, Bidford on Avon, Warwickshire, B50 4JH

Printed and bound by CPI Group (UK) Ltd, Croydon, CR0 4YY

www.grantabooks.com

For Jaume Vallcorba Plana

"…split up, and we will remain true to ourselves…"

—MARKUS WERNER, *ZÜNDEL'S EXIT*

TO THE BACK OF BEYOND

BY DAY you hardly noticed the hedge that separated the yard from that of the neighbors, it just seemed to merge into the general greenness, but once the sun went down and the shadows started to lengthen, it loomed there like an insuperable wall, until all light was gone from the garden and the lawn lay in shadow, an area of darkness from which there was no escape. Even now, in mid-August, it got cold quickly, and the damp chill seemed to pour out of the ground it had withdrawn into during the hours of sunshine, though even then it was never entirely gone.

Thomas and Astrid had put the children to bed, settled themselves with a glass of wine on the wooden bench outside the house, and divvied up the Sunday paper. After a while, Konrad's plaintive voice could be heard through the open window, and with a sigh Astrid had put down her section on the bench, emptied her glass, and gone inside without a word, not to reemerge. Thomas heard a soothing murmur and a little later saw the light come on in the living room. Then the window was snapped shut, a dry sound that signaled the end of the day, the weekend, the vacation. The light went out, and Thomas imagined Astrid crouching in the corridor, unpacking the big suitcase they had left there when they got back in the late afternoon. It must have been hot here too while they were gone, the house felt hot, the air was still and close, as though it stood under unusual pressure. Thomas went through the mail, which the neighbors had left out on the side table in the living room. Astrid was standing just behind him, even without seeing her he could feel her presence, her concentration. Nothing urgent, he said, and sat down at the table. Astrid threw open a few windows and said, as she went out, that she would get dinner ready. They had picked up a few items at a convenience store—bread, milk, cheese, a bag of lettuce. The kids had disappeared upstairs, Thomas could hear them bickering over something or other. When he and Astrid had taken them up to bed after dinner, Konrad had almost fallen asleep while brushing his teeth, and Ella hadn't even asked if she could read for a few minutes.

Thomas imagined Astrid making two separate piles of clean and dirty clothes. She carried the dirty things down to the utility room in the basement and put the clean ones away in the closet in the bedroom; the kids' things she folded neatly and left in a pile on the stairs to carry up tomorrow. She stopped for a moment at the foot of the steps and listened to a few quiet sounds from upstairs, the children getting comfortable in their newly made beds, in thoughts or dreams they were still at the beach, or maybe already back at school.

The light came on in Astrid and Thomas's bedroom, through the shutters it cast a pattern of stripes on the lawn, which had already lost all color with the onset of darkness. Astrid went into the bathroom, then out to the corridor again, to fetch the sponge bag out of the suitcase. She looked herself in the mirror with that blank expression with which she sometimes looked at Thomas. He used to ask her what she was thinking about, but she would invariably reply, Oh, nothing, and over the years he had begun to believe her and stopped asking.

Thomas folded up the newspaper and laid it on the garden seat. He picked up his glass, thinking he would finish it, then hesitated, rolled the wine around a few times, and set it down next to Astrid's empty glass, without having touched a drop. It was less a thought than a vision: the empty bench at dawn, the newspaper on it, sodden with dew, and their two glasses, the half-full one containing a few drowned fruit flies. The morning sun was shining through the glasses, leaving a reddish stain on the pale gray wood. Then the children emerged from the house and joined the straggle of other children on their way to school or kindergarten. A little later, Thomas left for work. He said hello to the old woman whose name he had once known but had now forgotten. He saw her out with her dog almost every morning; in spite of her age she had a vigorous walk, and a loud, confident voice when she said hello back to him, as though everything was fine and always would be. By the time he got home at lunchtime, the newspapers and the wineglasses would have been whisked away.

Thomas stood up and walked down the narrow gravel path that ran along the side of the house. When he got to the corner, he hesitated momentarily, then, with a bewildered smile that he was only half aware of, he turned away to the garden gate. He lifted the gate as he opened it, so that it didn't squeak, as he had done from when he was a boy, coming home late from a party, so as not to wake his parents. Even though he was stone cold sober, he had a sense of moving like a drunk, slowly and self-consciously. He walked down the road, past the neighbors' houses that got a little less familiar with each one he passed. There was light in some of the windows; it wasn't yet ten o'clock, but there was no one in the gardens or on the street. Ahead of him grew his shadow as cast by the streetlamp behind, then it merged in the light of the one following, which cast a fresh shadow behind him, which in turn grew shorter, overtook him, and hurried ahead of him growing all the while, a sort of ghostly relay of specters accompanying him out of the neighborhood, across the circular road, and into the business district that sprawled away from the village out into the flat land.

The doors of the big recycling plant stood open, and he could hear a monotonous drone. Thomas ducked as he passed, as though that would make him any less visible. When he got to the old industrial canal, he turned for the first time to look back, but there was no one to be seen, only the slightly quieter drone of the machines was still audible.

The road followed the canal for a while and then crossed a narrow bridge. Thomas accelerated, it was as though he had left the village's gravitational field and was now moving unimpeded through space, out into the unexplored terrain of night. The meadows either side of the road belonged to a horse breeder and were surrounded by tall fences. Right at the back of one of the meadows there were a few horses standing so close together that their bodies seemed to merge into a single many-headed form in the dark. The stables had no lights on. Just before Thomas reached them, he stopped to listen. When the children were smaller, he and Astrid had often walked this way; he couldn't remember now if the owners kept a dog or not. He hurried past the buildings. There was still no sound, but suddenly a halogen beam came on and lit up the yard and a portion of the road.

It was a relief to Thomas when he reached the edge of the woods. There was no moon in sight, and inside the woods, the gravel path was just a pale suggestion. Night seemed to draw him onward with its emptiness. The path carried on along the embankment, and then over the flood-protection barrier and to the far side of the narrow strip of wood. Here it was a little brighter. From the distance he could hear cars, and suddenly a locomotive. Thomas looked at his watch and with difficulty made out the time. It was half past ten, the train was punctual. For a moment he thought about the way the short line of carriages entered the brightly lit station, and the handful of passengers who got out walked through the underpass and to the bicycle racks, unchained their bicycles, and cycled off in every direction.

Now that Thomas was standing still, he noticed how quiet it was in the woods. Perhaps it was that that was giving him the sensation of not being on his own there. It was as though something was lurking in the darkness, neither man nor beast but a sort of unspecified life-form that took in the whole of the woods.

He walked on down the path to its end. From that point it was just another hundred yards across the meadow to the place where the canal joined the river at an acute angle. Thomas wandered over there; he used to light campfires and hang out there sometimes with his friends when they were teenagers. The canal seemed to have more water in it than the river, whose bed seemed almost dry. In spite of that, it would have been difficult to cross over to the other side. Thomas sat down on one of the rough stone slabs. There was a smell of rising damp from the river. He took out his cigarettes and with his fingertip felt how many he had left. Eleven. He lit one and looked up at the sky, which was now completely dark. It was a clear night, but there weren't many stars to be seen. He went through his pockets to see what he had with him: a key ring with a tiny torch, a pen-knife, dental floss, a lighter, and a cotton handkerchief. By the light of the torch, he counted his money; it came to more than three hundred francs. He shivered and briefly wondered about making a bonfire. Then he decided to go on, back to the little pedestrian footbridge, and then follow the canal west.

The narrow planked bridge felt wet and slithery under-foot. Thomas held on to the rail so as not to slip. He struck a footpath that was so narrow it gave him the feeling he was being gripped and passed on in complete darkness by the shrubbery to either side, to a gravel road that led straight through the woods for a quarter of a mile and then as far again across open pasture. Ahead of him he saw two cars speed across the road bridge, brush the houses on the far side with their conical beams, and disappear behind the hill. As he reached the road, he heard another car in the distance. He hid in the tall roadside grass and waited. The car sped past him. When he heard nothing more coming, Thomas jumped up and jogged across the bridge. He left the main road before the village and took a side road that followed the river to a glider airfield and beyond. When he was little, they had sometimes bicycled out here to watch the gliders, but it had never really interested Thomas, he just stayed for the sake of his friends, who had dreams of one day becoming pilots.

At the edge of the grass runway was a long hangar, and behind it, in the lee of a hedge, a dozen or so trailer homes, of which Thomas could only see the outlines. There weren't any lights anywhere, or any sounds to be heard. He was feeling very tired. He walked up to the nearest trailer, groped for the door handle, and turned it cautiously. It was locked. The other trailers were locked as well, but one had an awning that was easily opened. When Thomas stepped inside, he could feel there were duckboards over the ground. The air smelled stale, a smell of grass and old plastic and something gone off. By the feeble light of his little torch he saw a camping table and chairs and an improvised kitchen with a two-ring gas burner and a sink. In a corner was a ground cloth of stiff layered material. Thomas rolled himself up inside it and lay down on the ground, but even so he felt cold. He couldn't get to sleep on the hard floor, and he thought of home, wondering whether Astrid would have noticed his absence yet. She often went to bed ahead of him and didn't wake up when he came to bed.

When Astrid realized that Thomas wasn't lying beside her, she would suppose he was already up, even though she almost invariably got up first. She would go upstairs half asleep and wake the children and go downstairs again. Ten minutes later, freshly showered and in her robe she would emerge from the bathroom and call the children, who were bound to be still in bed. Konrad! Ella! Get a move on! If you don't get up now, you'll be late. Always the same sentences, and always the same replies too. One more minute. I'm up already. I'm just coming. On the way into the kitchen, Astrid would dart a look into the living room and wonder that Thomas wasn't there either. But these first forty-five minutes of the day always followed such a rigid plan that there wasn't a moment for her to think about anything else except what had to be done next. Switch on the coffee machine, add water, set the table, put out bread, butter, jam and honey, milk and cocoa. She shouted to the children once more, louder this time and with a note of anger, and she poured herself a first cup of coffee, which she drank standing up. Then at last the children came clattering downstairs and sat down. Konrad rubbed the sleep from his eyes, Ella set an open book next to her place, and Astrid had to tell her twice before she shut it and sulkily spread jam on a piece of bread. Then, finally, with mouth full, Konrad asked, Where's Papa? He had to leave extra-early today. Astrid had no idea what made her say that. It just seemed like the simplest thing, and even as she said it, it became a sort of fact. He had to go to the office early. The children didn't ask any more questions, even though Thomas hardly ever left the house before breakfast. Astrid tried to think whether Thomas had said anything about some appointment or something, but by then the children were getting up, and she needed to see that they didn't forget anything. Do you have swimming today? Put your sandals on. No, you'll need a pullover, it's quite cool outside. Leave the book here. Off you go! She kissed them on the cheek and pushed them out the door. For a split second she stood in the doorway, watched them go, saw them disappear around the corner, heard the familiar creak of the garden gate and the crash as it banged shut. There was fall in the air already.

As Astrid went into the bathroom to blow-dry her hair, she wondered about maybe going to the pool today. She had to do the laundry, finish unpacking, shop. She drew up a plan. The next time she thought about Thomas was when she left the bathroom. She called his office. His secretary said he hadn't arrived yet, and asked if they'd enjoyed the vacation. Oh, lovely, yes. Would you mind checking in his desk diary for me. No, said the secretary after a pause, there's nothing here. The first thing he has down is this afternoon, a meeting with a client. Will you ask him to call me quickly when he gets in then, said Astrid.

She bicycled off to the shops, hung the washing out to dry, and finished unpacking the suitcases. One of them contained a plastic bag full of shells that the kids had picked up on the beach. When Astrid tipped them onto the table, sand trickled out of the bag. She put the shells and snail shells in a flat basket, and carefully brushed the sand together, avoiding scratching the table. Then she stowed the suitcases in the attic. It was hot up there, the air had a consistency almost of cotton wool. Astrid thought a little ruefully of the past two weeks they had spent by the sea, the heat that she loved, the Spanish street markets, the wonderful fruit and vegetables, the astonishing array of fish and seafood you could get. Let's just stay here, Thomas had said flippantly on one of their last days. She had laughed and then they had stopped and considered it, spending the whole year by the sea. It was only a game, but in Thomas's eyes and the kids' Astrid could see a gleam of enthusiasm. And what would we live off? We could make jewelry out of shells and sell it on the promenade. What about school? Papa can homeschool us. Finally Astrid had said, But home is nice too. The sea would stop being special if it was always just outside the front door. And I'm sure they have winter storms here and the house would get damp, and there's not even any proper heating. She had always been the voice of reason in the relationship, and in the family. Sometimes she asked herself if Thomas would have chosen a different sort of life if they hadn't been a couple.

Thomas did not call. Perhaps he had tried while she was in the shops and hadn't wanted to leave a message. Or he had just plain forgotten. He was bound to have a lot on his plate after the vacation, and would have a hundred and one things to think about. Astrid felt too embarrassed to call the secretary again. She decided she would go for a quick swim after all. While on vacation she had resolved to take more exercise, to swim while the weather held, and then to take up jogging again.

On the radio they had predicted showers and falling temperatures for the afternoon, but there was little sign of that. Even so, the pool was practically empty. To Astrid it felt like a privilege to be able to go swimming in the middle of the day, even as she felt excluded by the more active world in which Thomas featured, and the children as well now, sitting at school racking their brains about math problems or writing an essay about what they had done on holiday. She had a guilty conscience, but that twinge of guilt had something pleasing too. The changing rooms were dirty, there was rubbish everywhere, and the pale blue concrete floor felt sticky underfoot. It must have been very busy here yesterday, the last day of summer, maybe the last warm day all year. After two weeks of swimming in salt water, she felt particularly heavy in the pool, as though something were dragging her down. She stopped after ten lengths and lay in the sun for a while, until her swimsuit felt a little dry. By half past eleven she was back home.

She took in the mail, glanced at the paper, and hung up the last of the wash. She had promised the kids their favorite meal, pancakes with applesauce and Nutella. While she mixed the batter, she had the radio on, though she only ever got mad at the chirrupy hosts who talked nothing but nonsense and treated the callers who rang in with the answer to some quiz question as though they were idiots.

The kids were late back. For five weeks they hadn't seen their friends, and they would have had a lot to talk about on the way home. Ella gave her a curt greeting and went into the living room. As Astrid set the table, Ella sat on the sofa, reading. What was school like? Ella mumbled something incomprehensible. In the kitchen, Astrid caught Konrad just tearing off a strip of pancake and pushing it in his mouth. Hands off! she called. Can't you wait? Where's Papa? asked Konrad. He won't be back for lunch today, he's got too much to do. All the more pancakes for us, then, said Konrad.

Over lunch the children talked about what their classmates had got up to during vacation. Astrid listened absently. She wondered what the story was with Thomas. She managed to calm herself down. What was it going to be? The evening before he'd been the way he always was. It wasn't as though anything unusual had happened during vacation either, on the contrary, the two weeks had been unusually harmonious. Most of the time they'd been on the beach or in the holiday rental. The drive back had been a strain, twice they'd been caught in traffic in France, but Thomas wasn't one to get too worked up about things like that. He was pretty even-tempered altogether, just a regular Joe, as he sometimes said himself. There was bound to be some perfectly ordinary explanation for his absence. Astrid didn't even feel worried.

That afternoon the kids went back to school, and Astrid did some work in the yard. After weeks of neglect, the garden looked pretty wild, the weeds ankle-high and the tomato plants tangled like nobody's business. Astrid weeded and tied the tomatoes, and pinched some of the buds. From the west some dark clouds were approaching and covered the sun. Astrid mowed the lawn. The sound of the mower was unusually loud and echoey, almost as though she was in some enclosed space. She hadn't quite finished when she felt the first drops of rain. Hurriedly she took down the wash and carried it indoors. She put the lawn mower away in the basement, and threw open the shutters all over the house. In Konrad's room she stopped and looked out at the rain, which was falling diligently and almost noiselessly. It had grown cool; she shivered and closed the window. The house still felt warm, but it was no longer oppressive.

With the weather, Astrid's mood had changed as well. As she walked down the stairs, she thought of the kids who would soon be back from school and that she shouldn't have let them go without their raincoats. Their unprotectedness felt like an accusation. So many times she felt the need to protect Konrad and Ella from all sorts of things, from mean fellow pupils, unfair teachers, perfectly ordinary things that were part of any child's growing up, and she hadn't managed. The telephone rang. It was Thomas's secretary, saying she had tried a couple of times already. She sounded more upset than Astrid felt. There was a meeting scheduled for two o'clock, she said. I was in the garden, said Astrid. And then, she didn't know why, He's sick, I should have called to let you know, I'm sorry. The secretary seemed unsurprised that Astrid this morning had asked her if she'd seen Thomas and was now claiming he was at home. The ease of the explanation seemed to clear all cavils out of the way. To lend credence to her lie, Astrid explained that Thomas had a heavy cold. Perhaps it was the air conditioning in the car or just the exhaustion after the long drive. I had a bad catarrh the other week, said the secretary, and laughed as though she had made a joke. Do you suppose he will be in tomorrow? I don't think so, said Astrid. Well, I hope he gets over his vacation soon, said the secretary, laughing again, give him my best, won't you.

Astrid tried to distract herself by thinking about dinner, and what she would cook and how they would sit together in the warm dining room, while the rain fell outside. But suddenly she felt convinced that Thomas wouldn't be there for dinner either, or tomorrow. The feeling took her breath away, not concern but a crippling fear as though she already knew what would happen.

Thomas must have slept in spite of his uncomfortable bed. His back hurt and he felt cold. It was pitch-dark under the canopy, and even though he held his wrist against his face he couldn't tell what the time was. For a while he lay there and tried to go back to sleep, but the cold was so piercing that he finally crept out of his ground cloth and got up. It was a little lighter outside. There was a risen moon, almost full, though it seemed to be a long way off. Thomas walked past the hangar on the grassy landing strip, with thin shreds of mist hanging over it. It was easier to see out in the open, and he could make out the first glimmers of light to the east. He did knee bends until he felt warmer, then he went back to the trailer. It got light quickly. From the woods there was a confused concert of birdsong and, from the distance, cowbells and the occasional car on the country road the other side of the river.

He was hungry. He tried the doors of all the trailers once more, but they were all locked. He thought briefly about breaking into one, but he would have needed a tool to do that, and all he had was his little pocketknife, which was good for cleaning his fingernails or opening a letter but not much more. He was on the point of giving up when he noticed that a sash window was open in one of the trailers. With some effort he forced his arm through it and clicked the catch. The window was very small, and it surprised him that he was able to twist himself up through it.

Inside it felt cramped and there was a musty smell. The window Thomas had clambered in through was over a kind of sofa bed. After feeling around for a while, he managed to find the switch. A weak economy bulb shed gray light over the inside of the trailer. The walls and units were cladded with fake walnut paneling, the cushion material was purple-and-beige in an old-fashioned looking plaid pattern, crocheted curtains hung in the windows. Thomas threw open all the cupboards. One contained sticky bottles of oil and vinegar, an almost empty tube of mustard, various spices and flavorings, tea bags and instant coffee; in others there were pasta and rice, cans of tomatoes, packets of instant soup. Finally he found two packs of cookies and half a bar of chocolate. He ate the cookies and felt a bit sick, but at least he was no longer hungry. He turned out the light and opened the door. He was startled to find that it was completely light outside.

In the middle of the trailer park was a small fenced-in pool and next to it an open building, little more than a shelter, really. Inside, Thomas found showers, toilet stalls, and sinks. There was no warm water, but he took a quick shower anyway. The cold water was refreshing, and even though he had hardly slept that night, he felt very alert. He dried off perfunctorily on a stained towel that was hanging beside one of the sinks. Then he went back into the mobile home, pocketed the chocolate, took the empty cookie packages and threw them in the trash. He decided against the palaver of bolting the mobile home and scrambling out through the window. The next time the owners came by, they might be puzzled to find the door unlocked and the cookies gone, but they surely wouldn't suppose anyone had broken in.

Thomas walked on along the narrow road he had come down the day before. As far as the airfield, he had known every path, every meadow and patch of woods. But once outside the perimeter of his village, his mental map of the area grew vaguer and consisted of railway lines, principal roads and towns, and the number of blank spaces in between kept growing.

At the end of the airfield the strip of grass narrowed between the river and the woods. A few dozen yards away, three deer were grazing in the high grass. Thomas stopped. The deer lifted their heads and looked at him. Even though they were some way off, he could feel that they had spotted him. For a heartbeat they stood still, then with their strangely slow movements they ran off in the direction of the woods and disappeared among the trees. I'll be safer in the woods, thought Thomas, I need to get off this road. He still wasn't being sought, presumably Astrid wouldn't have remarked his disappearance yet, but he didn't want to run into anyone who would remember him later.

When he ran off in the night, he had instinctively headed west. Now for the first time he stopped to think which direction he should follow. If he continued along the valley, he would soon get to the city and areas with too much light, too many people, and a dearth of places to hide. Even at night he wouldn't be safe there. He needed to head south, into the hills, the mountains.

He followed a narrow gravel track that led into the woods and up the slope. But before long, it was curving around, back into the village. Thomas left it, and cut up through the steeply banking trees. There was a steady hum of traffic; the road was more clearly audible up here than from the airstrip. The birds had quieted down.

At the top the woods came to an end, and Thomas saw scattered farmhouses surrounded by fields and meadows, stately forms with large outbuildings and mighty silos. A little farther off was a small village, consisting of a handful of houses and a church, and behind that, on the horizon, a chain of wooded hills. Thomas walked down the narrow aisle of a maize field. The stalks were so tall that only their movement would have indicated his presence. After that, the country was open, meadows with occasional tall fruit trees and lower-growth wheat and beet fields. So as to draw the least attention to himself, Thomas followed footpaths. Once, when he saw a tractor approach, he stopped and looked around for a hiding place, but there was no cover anywhere. The tractor was being driven by a kid barely older than Ella, who greeted him with a nod of the head. Thomas replied as casually as he could.

He managed to get around the village, and came to a crossroads with a little wayside chapel and a large cross with a gilded Savior. He read the Bible verse on the pediment. All ye that pass by, behold and see if there be any sorrow like unto my sorrow. The chapel was locked, but through the barred windows he could see a couple of plain wooden pews and a small altar, decorated by fresh flowers. Thomas sat down on the sandstone steps outside. On the horizon he could see the hill on which his village was situated. He had come much less far than he had hoped. The safest thing would be to hide somewhere and wait for it to get dark, but he was afraid of losing his way, and he was scared too of dogs, which by night were still more unpredictable than in the daytime. He looked up at the sun to orient himself. Not long ago he had taught Konrad the old Boy Scout trick: point the hour hand of your watch at the sun, and south will be halfway between there and one o'clock.

The gently rolling country continued to rise, and before long, he was in another wood. There were raspberries growing at the edge of it, and Thomas picked a few. A chilly wind had got up that shook the boughs and caused the leaves to rustle. It was an airy, well-tended beech wood, the smooth trunks like pillars in a lot of space, their green canopy in continual motion, casting shifting shadow patterns on the ground. Thomas sat down on a pile of logs beside a logging road. The alertness he had felt after getting up was a memory, he was sleepy now, and exhausted, and unable to think clearly. When he heard footsteps, he fled into a little thicket of pines that felt like a tumor in the body of the wood. He hunkered down and only yards away a woman cantered by on horseback. She had to be roughly his age and sat bolt upright in the saddle, bouncing rhythmically up and down. Through the treetops, sun dogs fell on her slender form. For a moment Thomas had the feeling all was well. The only thing wrong and out of place in the harmonious scene was himself. He went deeper into the tangle of pines. Once he was quite certain that he could no longer be seen from the track, he lay down on the soft, pine-needle-strewn ground. He thought of Astrid as the equestrienne. She had ridden as a girl, there were photographs of it in her old albums. She looked confident and sure of herself, as though she was exactly where she wanted to be. It was that confidence and uprightness that Thomas had fallen in love with twenty-five years ago, even though (or maybe just because) he sensed that it cost her an effort to keep up the illusion. It was at moments of uncertainty, of crisis and quarrel, but also of sexual passion that he felt closest to her, and their love seemed to him as strong now as in the first months of their relationship. He wondered how long she would manage to keep the illusion going before she collapsed.

The children were in the living room, doing their homework. Astrid hadn't been able to stand being at the table with them and had gone upstairs. She was sorting through the clothes, folding things up and stowing them away in cupboards. She ironed Thomas's shirts. Briefly it crossed her mind that it was pointless, and the absurd notion came to her that what she was doing was wiping away his traces. Irritated, she shook her head. The warmth of the steam, the smell of the tidily stacked laundry calmed her. Everything was all right. She concentrated on her work, the collars, the shoulders, the back, the sleeves, the cuffs, and when they were done put the shirts away on hangers on a rail. They hung there like inert clones of Thomas. Once, Astrid thought she heard the doorbell. She set the iron down on the board and listened, but everything was quiet downstairs. She called down to the kids. Have you finished your homework? Konrad's bugging me, called Ella. Leave Ella alone, called Astrid. She heard Konrad climb the stairs. He stopped in the doorway. Have you finished your homework? I'm bored. Will you play with me? I need to fix dinner, said Astrid. Why don't you read something. Where's Papa, asked Konrad. He's not coming, said Astrid, he's gone away for a few days. She was surprised at the way Konrad, at the way everyone, seemed to accept her crude lies without a murmur. She seemed to be the only one who actually registered the fact that Thomas had disappeared. To begin with, there had been a kind of consolation in that, but the longer he stayed away, the more panicky she felt, and for moments at a time she had the sense she was going mad, she had only imagined it, and Thomas had never actually lived here, had never even existed.

While she got dinner ready, she listened to the evening news. Everything was the same as always, the calm voice of the newsreader, the crises dotted around the globe, the political intrigues, the triumphs and disappointments of athletes. Astrid set the table and called the children, who were sitting in front of the TV and only came when they heard a threatening note in her voice. Now Ella finally asked after her father, and Astrid repeated her lie, which cost her less difficulty; it was as though it had acquired some truth from being repeated. She was making herself Thomas's accomplice, it felt as though she was joined with him in some secret conspiracy. Papa had to go somewhere for a few days, he left very early this morning, that's why he couldn't say goodbye to you. Did he take the car? asked Ella. Astrid looked at her in astonishment, and said, Do you know, I don't know. I don't think so.

After she had put the kids to bed, she pulled on a sweater and a raincoat and went out into the garage. The car was there. Then she sat down on the bench outside, where, just twenty-four hours ago, she had sat with Thomas. The rain had stopped, but the temperature had dropped by twenty degrees from the day before, and she could feel the damp wooden bench through her jeans. She tried to reconstruct the evening. They had read the paper, she was given the living section and Thomas had the financial pages. Konrad had called, and she had gone inside to comfort him. He had asked her one of those questions whose only point was to detain her. She had spoken to him briefly and then kissed him good night. After that she had started to unpack the suitcases. She knelt down on the floor. When she got up, she felt giddy, and only then realized she was totally exhausted. She carried the dirty clothes down to the basement, went to the bathroom, brushed her teeth quickly, and got undressed for bed. She went into the bedroom in her underwear and took out a nightgown from the wardrobe. It was as though the fresh clean smell of it made her even more tired. Only when she was lying in bed did it occur to her that she hadn't said good night to Thomas, but he was bound to be up any moment. She couldn't even say for sure whether Thomas had come to bed at all that night or not. She had shaken out the duvet right after getting up, the way she always did. Later, she had come upon the newspaper and the wineglasses outside the house and carried them in, tipped out the end of wine where a few fruit flies had drowned, and rinsed the glasses, quickly scanned the parts of the paper she hadn't got around to reading the night before, and then put them with the rest of the recycling.

Astrid got up and walked to the garden gate. Without opening it, she looked up and down the street. Even though it wasn't yet dark, there was no one around. Most of the houses were inhabited by elderly people who she knew by sight, nothing more. She thought of going to look for Thomas, but she could hardly leave the children on their own, least of all at this time of day. For a long time she remained standing by the gate indecisively, then she went back inside. She picked up the phone, hesitated, called the police number, then set down the receiver. What would the police be able to do at this time of night? She would call them first thing in the morning. The idea of talking to someone else about Thomas's disappearance soothed her; even so, she lay in bed awake for a long time.

Thomas felt stunned when he woke up. It was only four in the afternoon, he thought he must have been asleep for longer. The thicket of pines turned out to have been a perfect hiding place, no one could have been there for years. But hiding wasn't any use to him now. He couldn't stay in the woods much longer; he wasn't hungry yet, but he was racked by thirst. He got up, brushed the pine needles off his clothes, and headed out of the woods.

The landscape here was on a bigger scale, the farms and pieces of forest were larger, the farmhouses no longer scattered but formed into little hamlets. For the first time Thomas had a long view, saw a series of hills in the distance, and beyond them in the haze the outline of real mountains. Dark clouds had drawn up, and Thomas put his best foot forward. The way was all downhill and he made rapid progress. He still didn't dare to walk along the roads, and took field tracks that involved him in frequent detours and doglegs. He was still worried about being found, he was only about fifteen minutes by car away from home, and he had customers who lived in these parts who would surely have spoken to him if he had run into them. They would have slowed to a stop alongside him and asked him where he was going and if he didn't want a lift. Later, they would remember where he had been when they met him, and what he had said.

It started to rain. The rain took a while to get heavier, and by the time Thomas started looking for shelter, he was already soaked. He didn't have a jacket, only the thin woolen sweater he had worn out of the house last night. His hair was plastered against his head, and he was shivering. He worried about catching cold. He walked on through the hilly landscape and got to a big wood. The trees, though, afforded barely any protection against the rain, and he didn't stop for long. As he emerged from the wood, he saw below him a slightly larger village than the ones he had so far passed. In the center around the church were some old half-timber buildings, while on the periphery were small light-industrial premises and apartment blocks. One slope was totally covered with identical sterile single-family housing. Right at the edge of the development was a large building with a gabled roof that looked like a hotel but seemed to be empty. The shutters were down over the windows, and the car park at the back was empty. The property was ringed by a high hedge. Maybe, Thomas thought, he could find shelter there until the rain stopped and it got dark. At least it should be easy to get in there, and to disappear again, if there did turn out to be someone home.

He followed a little lane steeply down, and when it turned into the village, crossed a newly mown pasture. The hedge behind the supposed hotel was scruffy and full of gaps. An old trailer was parked on the paved area that surrounded the building. A ramp led down to two garage doors, while a narrow flight of steps led up to a half-concealed back entrance. Thomas was struck by the great metal door with peephole that looked as though it had just been installed. All the while the house seemed to radiate a great sense of abandonment, so that even if he wouldn't have been able to explain why, he felt perfectly confident there was no one living there. The roof had a small overhang, enough to afford a little protection from the rain, which was now falling steadily. Thomas sat down on the top step and pulled out his cigarettes. The pack had gotten damp, the filters were full of water that got into his mouth as he drew on his cigarette and had a bitter taste. He got up and dropped the half-smoked cigarette into the ashtray by the door.

He remained sitting on the steps for a long time, unable to think what to do. He listened to the rain streaming down, the cars on the main road in front of the building, the tires hissing on the wet asphalt, and the village church striking one quarter then two. He remembered rain in his childhood, rain in his year of military service, rain in the summer vacations in the mountains, and it seemed as though all rain were one, a category all its own, quite separate from time.

He was tired, the only things that kept him from dropping off were the cold and the uncomfortable cement step he was sitting on.

A quiet creak directly over his head gave him a start. He looked up in alarm. The door was open and a woman in a leather miniskirt and fishnet stockings and a skimpy yellow top that exposed her midriff stood in the doorway, apparently just as alarmed as he was, though she recovered instantly. Yes? she said. Her voice sounded artificial, as though she had straightaway fallen into a practiced role. And who might you be? She lit a cigarette and started smoking it rapidly with nervous hands. After a few drags she dinched it in the ashtray and said, Why don't you come in? It's cozier. Without thinking, Thomas got up and followed the woman inside.

She led him along a red-lit passage into a large room with groups of easy chairs, a few tables, and a bar. There was a screen up near the ceiling; on it a young couple were arguing about something, but the sound was turned down so low that Thomas had no idea what it was about. At one of the small tables a couple of young women were knitting, one of them was in a robe, the other a shift that was so short he could see her panties. They glanced up at him and went on talking in a language that Thomas could neither understand nor identify. His guide had stepped behind the bar. Can I get you a drink? A glass of champagne? A beer? Do you have coffee? asked Thomas, and sat down on a barstool. Sure, said the woman. She took a thermos flask, poured two cups, and set them on the bar. Then she went back around the front and settled on the stool beside Thomas. I'm Amanda, she said, I'm from Hungary. She had an accent, though not a strong one. I was hiking, said Thomas, and got caught in the rain. We're not supposed to open until six, said the woman, but I'll make an exception for you. I just want to rest a bit, he said, and get my things dry. As though he had given orders, Amanda got up and went over to the table and joined the other women. The woman in the shift came across to Thomas and sat down beside him. She was blond, with pretty, girlish features. I'm Milena, I'm Romanian, she said, where are you from? She had a stronger accent than the other woman. Thomas gestured vaguely. How do you like Switzerland? he asked. I'm only here since one month, said Milena, before I work in club in Interlaken. Interlaken is pretty, said Thomas. Between two lakes, as the name suggests. Neither of them spoke. Milena smiled at Thomas and winked at him. Is this your first time here? Do you want a tour? Without waiting for him to answer, she got up and led him back out to the passage he had just come through. She opened a door to a room that had a big tub in the middle of it. This is our Jacuzzi, she said, in one hour you can go there with one or two girls. Sounds nice, said Thomas sheepishly. I show you my room, said Milena. She walked up a narrow flight of stairs, and he followed her as though he had no choice. Half an hour costs one hundred fifty francs, one hour is three hundred, anal is hundred more. We have loyalty card. If you buy six half hours, you get free blow job. Thomas had never been inside a brothel, and was bemused by the coolness with which she told him the prices. The businesslike tone had a certain charm, but he nevertheless said again he just wanted to rest for a while. Milena turned around, two steps above him. Her nipples made little bumps through the thin dress. She placed a hand on his shoulder and shimmied her hips slowly. You're all wet, she said, and smiled. You should take off your clothes.

I can give you massage. I am good. One hour is one hundred eighty francs, without penetration. She took Thomas by the hand, and drew him farther up the stairs. Don't be afraid. I won't bite you.

Breakfast without Thomas felt almost normal, but after the children were gone, Astrid went restlessly through the house, picking up things and setting them down again. In the kids' rooms she tidied a few toys away. She sat down at Ella's little schoolgirl desk and gazed absentmindedly at all the clutter, magazines, a game console, plastic figures, a handful of coins, glitter-ink pens, the signs of a life that as yet had few contours and therefore stood in need of these material props. Astrid wondered what there was for her to cling to. Her clothes and shoes? The few pieces of jewelry she owned? The albums with her girlhood snapshots? Somewhere in the attic there was a cardboard box of her old stuff, exercise books and drawings and this and that she had for some reason held on to. But those things didn't mean anything to her anymore, and when she ran into them from time to time they were less familiar to her than her children's things. More than once she had almost thrown out the whole box.

Last night, Astrid had decided she would go to the police; now she was afraid that if she took such a step it would make Thomas's disappearance permanent, an officially confirmed fact that would then remain part of her life from now on. Her hesitation had another reason that she was reluctant to admit to herself even though it was almost stronger than her fear. She felt shame. She would be seen going to the police station, and even if no one knew what it was about, it would become public knowledge at the latest when the missing person announcement appeared in the newspaper: Left home one night and not seen since. Anyone with any information is asked to get in touch with the cantonal police. Then everyone would know that Thomas had left, that he had walked out on her and the children, and tongues would wag and people would speculate about this and that. They would at one and the same time ostracize her and with their thoughts and their unspoken questions interfere in her life.

It was almost eleven before she at last got a grip on herself. Outside, it felt as though gravity had failed, with every step she felt so light she could have floated away. She was relieved not to run into anyone she knew. There were a few people standing around in front of the station, two women had set their shopping bags down on the ground and stopped for a chat, on the public benches there were some young people smoking, and at the newspaper kiosk an old man was filling in a lottery coupon. The faces all looked strangely distorted to her, like caricatures. Astrid was no longer part of their everyday world, in which only yesterday she had moved perfectly naturally. She was marked, even though no one knew about it yet.

Once, the police station had been down a quiet side street, but a couple of years ago it had been moved into a new building near the train station, next to a bakery and cafeteria. Astrid looked around worriedly before walking in. There was no one at the front desk. She sat down on a chair, and straightaway jumped up again. There was a poster on the wall about break-ins: No. 5, never go on holiday. A wire rack contained public-information leaflets about Internet bullying, going abroad, about burglar alarms and the right to bear arms. At last a woman arrived, a little older than Astrid, radiating a friendly calm. Astrid said she had come to report a missing person. The woman asked her two or three questions, and then called a colleague. Ruf, said the officer, what can I do for you. He appeared terribly young to Astrid, with a soft and shapeless face, like a child's. She would have much preferred to deal with one of those craggy old detectives she watched on TV, men with wrinkled, experienced faces, who wouldn't bat an eyelid when told the most terrible things. They shook hands, and the policeman led her into a small interview room with yellow walls. Astrid said again that she had come to report a missing person. Excuse me, said the policeman, I'll be back in a moment. The room was empty, apart from the two chairs and a desk with a computer and printer on it. The walls were bare. The window gave on to a tiny yard. The venetian blinds were like window bars.

The policeman came back with a sheaf of papers and sat down facing Astrid. Well, tell me all about it. She explained her husband had disappeared the night before last, and she had no idea where he might be. Almost all missing persons resurface within a few days, the policeman said with a steady voice, but I'll take down his details and put them in the system anyway. He put on a sober, almost sorrowful expression and looked at the form in front of him, as if he were seeing it for the very first time. Then in an offhand tone of voice he started going through it with her. He took the particulars of Astrid and Thomas, and wrote down the time and place of disappearance. He inquired after their marital status and any joint children, Thomas's job and rank, his state of health, and any distinguishing physical traits. Tattoos? Piercings? No, said Astrid, and almost laughed at the idea. A beard, a mustache? She shook her head. No distinguishing marks. What was he wearing? She tried to make a mental picture of Thomas, but the harder she tried, the more blurry he seemed to get. Chinos and a shirt, but what color? White? Or blue? A gray sweater? Glasses? She hesitated for a moment. No, she said at last. Thomas never wore glasses. She couldn't say how he was traveling, only that the car and his bicycle were still there. Nor did she know what he had with him. Money? Sure to. He carries his ID in his wallet, same with credit card and bank card. A key ring. Presumably cigarettes, a lighter, a cotton handkerchief. No, no weapons. She had the sense that Thomas was rigidifying as she described him, becoming unrecognizable, the image of a dead man.

The policeman looked up from the form and into Astrid's eyes. There was a brief pause, as though a new chapter were beginning in the conversation, then he said, and his voice suddenly was very intense, I must ask you this: Could you imagine your husband has harmed himself? Astrid shook her head. No, absolutely not. He would never do such a thing, she said irately. Did he have money difficulties or other worries or anxieties? No. Did you fight at all during the last few days? We just got back from holiday, she said, as though that answered his question. We were in Spain. On the beach. It was very nice. We didn't quarrel, quite the opposite. I haven't the least idea why he's disappeared. She stopped for a moment, before adding, as though surprised about it herself: In fact we've never really had any arguments. As though he hadn't heard her answer, the policeman asked if they owned a holiday home or apartment, and when she said no, if she happened to have a recent photograph of her husband with her. Something else she hadn't thought of. I wouldn't mind taking a look around your house, if you've no objection, said the policeman. It's an odd thing, but you quite regularly get people hiding at home. Then while I'm there perhaps you could give me a photo of him.

He must have sensed Astrid's hesitation when he held open the door of the patrol car for her. If you prefer, we could take the other car, it is less obtrusive. Astrid told him the address and gave him directions during the drive, although he seemed to have no trouble finding the house. He parked on the roadside and got out. It's nice here, he said, as Astrid led him down the garden path to the door. I haven't uploaded the vacation pictures yet, she said, and walked into the lounge. The policeman stopped in the corridor and asked if it was all right if he took a look around. Shall I take my shoes off? No, said Astrid. She couldn't imagine a policeman in stockinged feet getting results.

She took the card out of her camera and transferred the pictures onto the family laptop, which was mostly what the children played games on. She looked over the pictures, but most of them were of Ella and Konrad. In one shot you could see Thomas and Konrad from behind, racing into the sea, another was of a massive paella pan that Astrid had taken in a restaurant, and you could see the bottom half of Thomas's face, with a rather strange half smile. Then she went through the pictures of the skiing holidays, Christmas, and last year's summer vacation, but there was not one proper shot of Thomas. Perhaps he had deliberately avoided being photographed and leaving traces in their shared life, evidence that could be used against him later on.

At long last she found a photograph from a Sunday walk that Konrad or Ella must have taken. It wasn't absolutely in focus, but Thomas looked very lifelike and alive in it. He was smiling, looking as though he had just said something and was waiting for a reply. She printed the picture on the little photo printer that Thomas had given her for Christmas, after she had complained about the way all the pictures might as well be locked up in the computer because no one ever looked at them.

Hearing the policeman walking down the stairs, she went out into the corridor. Is this the way down to the basement, he asked, pointing to the basement door. Don't bother, he said, as Astrid made a move to accompany him downstairs, and it suddenly dawned on her what he was doing. He didn't really believe that Thomas was hiding anywhere but that he might have committed suicide, maybe hanged himself in the basement or the attic. She shuddered at the idea, and even though she felt quite sure that Thomas would never harm himself, she stood there with pounding heart until the policeman came back up and shook his head in apparent relief. Nope. Nothing.

He wouldn't have a cup of coffee, just a glass of water, which he left untouched. He examined the photograph. I'd really like it if you could send me this as an attachment, he said, and gave her an e-mail address. Will it appear in the newspaper? Astrid asked. She felt ashamed of the question, but it was one she had to ask. No, replied the policeman, we'll just put it in our inquiries file. Anytime he produces his passport, either at a frontier or in the course of a traffic control, my colleagues will draw his attention to the fact that he's being sought. Then, if we get his consent, we'll be able to tell you his whereabouts. Is that it then? asked Astrid. An adult has the right to disappear, said the policeman. If there was a suggestion of criminality or self-harm, then we could track him with a dog. But after thirty-six hours have elapsed that's not a straightforward matter. What about the children, asked Astrid, what do I tell them? As I say, most missing persons tend to surface after a few days, he said, and got up. And with that he drank his water too, all in one gulp. Ruf, he said, at your service, and gave Astrid his card, after they had shaken hands and she muttered something. You're welcome to call anytime. Will I get put through to you directly? she asked. Sure, if I'm on duty. He took the card and wrote his mobile number on the back. There. In case of emergencies, he said.

After he left, Astrid wept for the first time. She sat at the table that still had the photograph of Thomas on it and cried, quietly to begin with, then loudly. Her body shook, it was a while before her sobbing eased and started coming at longer intervals. Once she had finally calmed herself, she went to the bathroom and splashed cold water on her face. She put the printed photograph of Thomas away in a drawer.

Thomas was sitting in the darkest corner of the bar. Gradually the place had filled up. Half a dozen men were standing or sitting around, talking with the girls or going off with them down the red corridor, to return half an hour later. There was a couple as well. The woman was of an almost severe beauty that looked out of place. She had black hair and a very pale complexion, and was wearing a denim skirt and a white floppy blouse. She was standing next to one of the men who wasn't looking at her, and was in negotiations with one of the prostitutes. Thomas wasn't able to interpret the expression on her face, she seemed at once alarmed and very attentive. When shortly afterward she followed the prostitute and the man out of the bar, she looked back over her shoulder, as though to form a detailed impression of the scene for later. Thomas lowered his head and shut his eyes. The music was loud and so monotonous that he was no longer aware of it. He went up to the bar for another beer, even though he no longer had the money to pay for it. And when any child could have told you that you shouldn't use plastic if you were trying to disappear. Sooner or later, Astrid was bound to go to the police, and the police would ask her about money movements in their joint account. The thought gave him a sense of security. He pictured himself lying in bed next to Astrid, not touching, but he could feel her warmth and heaviness, as though the two of them were two stars, held by mutual gravity, orbiting round and round each other, without ever getting closer.

Thomas felt his shoulder being shaken, and for an instant it was as though that was the only thing there was in the world, this mild motion that was spreading like a wave, eventually going through his entire body. When he opened his eyes, a young man was standing at his table. He had curly black hair and a wide contemptuous sneering expression. Tired? he asked. Just a bit, said Thomas. He must have been asleep because the bar was almost empty. You'd better go home then, said the man, come back to us when you're feeling a bit more like it. Although the man's tone wasn't unpleasant, he made it sound like an order. Thomas went up to the bar and paid with his card. He had only had two bottles of beer, and yet he was staggering slightly. When he turned to leave, he saw the young man still had his eyes on him. In the cloakroom he hesitated briefly before taking a coat at random off the peg, it was a dark green waxed jacket, and quickly left the premises. Only now did he look at his watch, it was already past one. The rain had stopped, but the streets were still wet. There were no lights on in any of the village houses, just a couple of streetlamps giving a murky illumination. Thomas walked down the main street and quickly left the village behind him. After a few hundred yards, he stopped and went through the pockets of the jacket he had picked up. He found a lighter and a ballpoint, a packet of herbal sweets, a couple of receipts, some loose change, a pocket calendar, and an empty spectacle case. He held on to the calendar, the ballpoint, the money, and the lighter, and dumped the rest of the things.

After about half an hour he was on a wider road. Now he knew where he was. Once he had made his way through the little town he was on the edge of, he would enter sparsely inhabited woodland, where he would feel safe. From time to time a car came along, but it was so quiet that Thomas could hear the sound of the motor a long way off and was able to conceal himself behind a hedge or the corner of a building.

He followed the road into the town center, where there was a small pedestrian zone. He walked down a shopping street, looking for something to eat. Some time ago, he had come across an article in the newspaper about people who lived perfectly well from scavenging the trash containers of supermarkets, but all there was here were fashion and shoe shops, a jeweler's, a sports and fitness store, and a bakery. When he finally saw a supermarket, he found the niche with the ramp where the containers stood locked behind a grate, like the entrance to a fortification.

The dead town had something ghostly about it. Thomas had a notion that all the inhabitants had hit the road as he had and left everything the way it happened to be. He was reminded of a book he had read as a child and never forgotten. In it, almost everyone on earth had been turned to stone, the only survivors a group of children, and they were traveling around the world in an airship. After some time they ran into another group of survivors and fought them to the death. Thomas remembered how the ending had disappointed him. If it had been up to him, then the journey around the deserted planet could have gone on forever and ever.

At the station, there was a vending machine, and Thomas bought himself candy bars, bags of chips, and sugary drinks until he had no more change. He bundled up his purchases in his sweater. Next to the machine was a display of a map of the town, plus a hiking map of the surrounding area. He memorized the way he needed to take as well as he could.

The road led him out of town through an industrial zone, over fields and meadows and through a couple of small villages that had almost grown together. His feet were hurting him by now, but Thomas carried on. The valley narrowed, and after a while he reached a group of buildings, a psychiatric clinic he knew of by name. Here too everything was dark and silent. In the middle of the buildings, there was a solitary light next to a small pavilion. He saw a plan of the institution, with all the various wards and workshops and dormitories marked in. But all the paths ended at the edge of the map, as though the clinic was on an island that no one could leave. Thomas remembered the road he had seen on the station hiking map, and walked through the institute and up a slope toward a wood, even though the little road was marked as a dead end. As he passed a multistory building, he saw a light on in a ground-floor window. A woman was sitting in front of a computer, presumably on night duty. She had her head lowered, maybe she was reading, in a world of her own. The first time Thomas met Astrid, in the bookstore, she had kept on recommending books to him that he read for her sake, but he was never really a reader, the artificial world of books had never really come alive for him. In fact, the older he got, the less he seemed to feel the need to be diverted or entertained.

At the edge of the wood, the asphalt road became an unpaved forest track that was wide enough for him to be able to follow it easily in the dark. Thomas had the sensation of entering a different sort of space. He could hear the pouring of water, which first grew louder, then, as the track started to climb, softer again. He heard an occasional cracking sound, otherwise there was silence. In the middle of the wood he discerned the outline of a massive concrete structure, presumably an army munitions dump. The terrain flattened out. Thomas felt relieved when he emerged from the wood; he had the sense of having escaped a danger. For some time already, he had heard cowbells. Now they were very close, and he saw the dark forms of cattle on the pasture. The sound came closer, the animals must have sensed him, and now they came bounding up to him in wild leaps. Thomas worried the clanging bells might wake the farmer, but when he passed the house, there was no light. Not even a dog barked at him.

Walking felt easier now, though his feet still hurt. The little track led slightly downhill through fenced-in pastures and then up toward a round knoll. Thomas decided to stop there and rest. The grass was cut short, but it was wet either from rain or early dewfall. He felt the moisture through his shoes. At the summit was a group of trees. He sat down in the grass and looked around. The stars were densely packed in the wide sky. Lights flickered in the distance. Only when Thomas made out mountain peaks at the edge of the horizon did he get his bearings. He ate two bags of potato chips and a candy bar. The mashed-up food made a disgusting pulp in his mouth. He swilled it down with a Coke. He pressed and carefully folded the packaging, and put it with the empty bottle back in the bundle with the rest of his provisions.

In the east the moon was rising, a dark orange disk looming very close. The higher it climbed, the smaller it seemed to get. At the same time its illumination grew stronger, and before long, a milky shimmer lay over the whole landscape. Thomas was too tired to be able to go on. He lay down in the grass and rolled himself up like a kid. It wasn't cold, but the damp got into his clothes. He thought of home, of Astrid and the sleeping children, who already seemed to be so far away, it was as though he had been gone for weeks.

The children came home from school a little after four, first Ella and a little after her Konrad, who tended to dawdle. Ella was already sitting at the living-room table doing her homework when he walked into the kitchen and mutely hugged his mother. Astrid liked those moments when he was as affectionate as he'd been as a small child. In spite of that, she freed herself from his hug and asked him if he had any homework. I'm hungry. Then eat an apple, she said, and called into the living room, Do you want one, Ella? She cut up two apples in slices, put them on two little plates, and handed Konrad one, taking the other to Ella. She looked over Ella's shoulder and read the opening lines of the piece she was writing in her exercise book. Something that happened during my holidays, was the title, but Ella was writing about the stray dogs she had seen on the beach. One of the dogs was very sweet and terribly affectionate. I don't know what breed he was. My father said he's a mungrel, which are the best kind of dogs, because they're a bit of everything. I badly wanted to take him home with us, but my mother said we weren't allowed to take dogs across the border.

One of the many untruths she had recourse to every day with the children, thought Astrid. At lunch, she had claimed that Thomas was eating with a client, and the children didn't even ask, as though they had failed to notice that their mother's explanations were contradictory. They had been unusually quiet, in fact, almost somehow inhibited. Astrid took an apple slice off Ella's plate and put it in her mouth. Hey, said Ella, that's mine. Mongrel has an *o* in it, said Astrid, the first vowel.

While she got dinner ready, she thought she wouldn't be able to fob the children off with such threadbare versions for much longer. But what was she going to say to them instead? Your father has disappeared? And anything beyond that? She herself didn't know what had happened. Surely nothing had befallen him. He just had to go, leave. Maybe that was the explanation. He didn't have another woman, hadn't embezzled any money, hadn't run up debts he was unable to repay. He hadn't done himself an injury, he had simply walked away. It was an urge she had felt herself. When Ella was very young and colicky, and hadn't slept through a single night, when she stayed up screaming for hours, and Astrid was tired to the point of exhaustion, she had sometimes walked out of the house, leaving the baby all alone for half an hour or even an hour sometimes. She had gone to the station and sat down on a bench on a platform and just taken deep breaths. A train arrived, people got on and off. Astrid stood up, walked toward the train. The doors closed, the train moved off, and Astrid sat down again. Then she imagined coming home, it was silent, ghostly silent. Finally she had gone home, and Ella was still screaming, red-faced with exertion, and Astrid had picked her up out of her crib, and carried her around the house, and whispered to her until she calmed down a little. Astrid had never said a word to Thomas about these escapades; she was ashamed of them. Maybe he had such fantasies of flight as well, and needed time alone to collect himself in the din of their normal day. The policeman was surely right, Thomas would come back soon, and they would resume their previous life, only a little unsettled by the knowledge that there was nothing natural or inevitable about it, and that sometime one or other of them might get lost for a while or even forever.

For once, the children set the table uncomplainingly. Over dinner, they were silent again. Finally Astrid said, Your father's gone away, I have no idea where he is or when he'll come back, but I'm sure he won't stay away for much longer. Is he dead then? asked Ella. Astrid looked at her in alarm. No, of course he isn't, how could you say that? Ella jumped up from the table and ran away. Astrid followed her upstairs and found her rolled up on her bed, crying. She lay down behind her and wrapped her in her arms and said, I'm quite sure your papa's fine. He just needed some time by himself after the holiday.

I'm sure he'll be back soon. Quite sure. Ella didn't say anything, but she seemed to calm down gradually. After a while, Astrid said, I'd better go downstairs and see what Konrad is up to. Are you all right now? Ella nodded.

Konrad was still sitting at the table, on his plate was a piece of bread that he had cut up into little cubes. Why did Papa go away? he asked. Astrid sat down beside him and laid her hand on his shoulder. Sometimes people just want to be by themselves. You're like that sometimes too, remember? When you lock yourself up in your room. Now finish your dinner. Can I play my computer game then? asked Konrad.

It was daybreak when Thomas awoke. The moon was high, but it didn't shed much light in the brightening sky. The group of trees that Thomas had seen as an outline the previous night were just a few sick specimens with leafless crowns, their trunks a tangle of ivy. A sweetish smell hung in the air.

Thomas's clothes were sodden, but he didn't feel cold. He rubbed his hands on the damp grass and wiped the sleep from his eyes. Then he picked up his bundle and headed on in a southerly direction. There was no one around anywhere, and he walked along field tracks, always mindful not to lose his bearings.

The track he was following led along the edge of a meadow, getting steadily fainter, until it finally came to an end in a rough and ready turning circle at the edge of a wood. Thomas carried on into the wood, which consisted mainly of conifers. The sweetish scent was even more pronounced here — it was as though the air was suffused with honey. The gradient fell away steeply. He thought he could still make out the path a short distance away, zigzagging down into a gully, but then even these last vestiges of it disappeared, and Thomas made the bulk of the descent on the seat of his pants. At the bottom of the gully he had to force his way through thick ferns and bushes. He had spiderwebs smeared on his hands and face. He recognized some plants and was surprised he could remember their names, which his father had taught him when he was a boy: horsetail, herb paris with its blue-black fruit, stinking storksbill, and woodbine with its doubled-up red berries that looked almost like red currants but that he knew were poisonous. He heard a loud rushing sound, and farther below him he saw a waterfall that tumbled a few meters over a pile of conglomerate into a small pool.

Directly above the waterfall was a shallow where Thomas was able to get across. He took the opportunity to wash again and drank some of the water, scooping it up with his hands.

The opposite side of the gorge was even steeper. Thomas had to pull himself up by roots and little saplings. He kept losing his footing. By the time he finally reached level ground, his pants were filthy and he had lost an hour without very much to show for it.

The sky, which had previously been no particular color, now turned blue. A few little clouds burned a reddish yellow in the slanted low light, and when its beams touched the woods and meadows, the whole scene began to glow. Thomas sat down in the grass at the edge of a small, unmown meadow, surrounded on three sides by trees, and finished the provisions he had bought at the station.

When he emerged from the shelter of the trees, he saw not far away a village consisting of a score or so of farmhouses. There was no one to be seen, and a little nervously he approached and walked through it. The gate of one of the cowsheds stood open. Inside, a woman was connecting the cows up to the milking machine. A transistor radio was going, and Thomas heard the perky voice of the host, and the opening bars of a country tune. He walked on quickly, past a cheesery, from where he heard a clatter of metal and the rushing sound of water, over the same tune he had just heard from the cowshed. The narrow street led up to a height, from where Thomas had his first view of the peak of Säntis and the Churfirsten mountains, gleaming in the morning sun. He turned to look back at the idyllically tidy little village below him. How much sweat was needed to maintain this tidiness, to get up early every morning and do the same unvarying tasks, to milk the cows, to clean their shed, to fertilize and mow the pastures, and to bring in the hay. The work might have gotten easier through the mechanization of the past hundred years, but it wasn't the physical effort he was thinking of so much as the optimism, the faith, the conviction that it was the right thing to do. He too had once formed part of this quiet consensus, he had functioned in the way that was expected of him, without it ever having been discussed. He had gone to school for nine years, completed a traineeship, done his military duty, and then gone back to being a trainee. He had married Astrid, had kids, moved into his parents' old house, and slowly, over time, done it up. It had taken persistence and willpower, but now they were living there in the house, which was slowly falling down, imperceptibly but unstoppably. He had read somewhere that a building wasn't finished until it had collapsed into ruins. Perhaps the same was true for human beings.

Every day Thomas went to the office and did his job; he kept the books for his clients, produced their year-end accounts, and filled out their tax returns. Some of the businesses failed; either the market changed or the people made mistakes or they lacked entrepreneurial spirit, but most of them managed to get through life without any major calamities, achieved a certain degree of comfort, and eventually went into retirement. Then they would sit in his office—the carpenter or the auto mechanic or the butcher and his son, who was to take over his father's business. They would talk about money, about accommodations and inventories and investments that needed to be made, but never about what really mattered. What was it all for? In the course of their daily exertions, there was never a moment when they could ask themselves such questions; maybe they were scared of them, or they had understood that such questions were impossible to answer and hence should not be asked at all. Thomas was unsure whether to admire or despise them.

In the next village, which was a little bigger, there was already a fair amount of activity, cars driving through the streets, children headed off to school, and outside the general store stood a supply van. Thomas tried to steer clear of the center. Hikers were nothing out of the ordinary in these parts, but the thing was he probably looked like a tramp—he was unwashed, his clothes were filthy, and he didn't have anything like a rucksack or trekking poles.

He passed an apple orchard, but the apples that were lying in the grass were still unripe. Under an expanse of black netting he found a bilberry patch. The gate in the fence was not locked, and he walked in and picked a few handfuls of the berries, which were far bigger and sweeter than those he remembered picking in the mountains as a child. He heard engine noise coming nearer. Still hungry, he crept out.

Next to one of the farmhouses a few alpacas were grazing and looked at him with their enormous eyes. They had faces like comic animals. Do not feed! it said on the fence that enclosed the pasture, and next to the sign a metal box with a lid that contained bread for the animals. Thomas opened it, and stuffed a few slices of the stale bread in his pocket.

His way now took him pretty sharply downhill through a group of new houses that were a strange cross between farm-houses and single-family homes. Swings and trampolines and wading pools sat on the trimmed lawns. There was a closed restaurant in the narrow valley and a sawmill, behind whose windows fouled with spiderwebs and dust no one seemed to be working. Between the road and the stream a few sawn-up tree trunks were stacked to dry. Farther down, where a nar-row pool had formed against a small dam, Thomas stripped behind a pile of boards and dipped into the freezing-cold water. He washed himself, and rinsed the worst of the dirt out of his clothes and hung them up on the branches of an elderberry. Then he dunked the stale bread in the stream water. It tasted watery and fell apart in his mouth, but it at least filled his belly and, having eaten, he felt better. Stark naked he lay down in the sun to rest.

Although it had gotten chilly, Astrid went back outside once the children were in bed. She took the paper with her and a glass of wine, and sat down on the bench in front of the house. Just two days earlier, exactly forty-eight hours, she had sat there with Thomas. If she shut her eyes now, she could imagine he was sitting beside her. From inside she could hear Konrad's plaintive voice. Will you go to him? she asked. Oh, just leave him be, said Thomas, he'll stop by himself. Will you please, she repeated, and with a groan he got up and went inside. Shortly afterward, she could hear him talking with Thomas, and the two of them laughing. Go to sleep now, Thomas called from the top of the stairs. Then the light came on in the living room, and Thomas put his head out the window. Are you coming in now? In a minute, said Astrid. She heard him shut the window, and had the brief sensation that he was a very long way away. She pictured him going to the cellar for a bottle of wine. He checked the level of heating oil in the boiler, and worked out whether it was enough to see them through the next winter or if they would have to order more. When he came out of the cellar, he glanced at the thermometer that indicated the out-door temperature, sixty, but it was due to warm up again in the next couple of days. Then Astrid heard the calming tones of the TV, sounds and voices, music. She set down the paper, remained sitting for a minute longer, as though biding her moment, then got up and left the garden. She looked up and down the street, as though it might offer some clue or prompt, but she didn't see anything out of the ordinary, just the nocturnal street with its line of single-family homes. She saw Thomas, equally perplexed, standing in the street, uncertain which way to go. Once a week he played handball and afterward would drink a few beers with his teammates; other than that he spent almost every evening at home. Ear-lier on, he sometimes had gotten together with a friend from his boyhood, but ever since the man joined the Unitarians and would talk about nothing else, Thomas had allowed the friendship to lapse. Astrid briefly wondered whether to call him, but she was sure that even in some extremity Thomas would never have turned to him, and apart from that man, there was no one she could think of to whom he might have gone. He had no close friends; his superficial relationships to colleagues at work, his clients, and his teammates seemed to be enough for him. Neither of them had an especially active social life, and since the children, they hardly ever went out in the evenings. Astrid had sometimes encouraged Thomas to meet up with his old friends again, but he seemed not to feel the need. I've got you, he would always say. Nor was he close to his parents or his sister, although they seemed to get on okay. If Astrid didn't remind him of their birthdays, he would probably have forgotten them as well.

Only then did she realize that tonight was Thomas's handball evening. The team practiced in a school gym just a couple of hundred yards away. She popped back inside the house and listened for the children. Hearing no sounds, she pulled on a coat and shut the door quietly after her.

The gym was half underground. Astrid stood in front of one of the plate-glass windows and looked down where the handball team was training, as they did every Tuesday. Most of the men were stood in a line. They seemed to be practicing a particular game situation, getting the ball thrown to them by the coach, hurling it into a corner of the goal, and joining the back of the line. Astrid scanned the line for Thomas, but of course he wasn't there. From where she stood, the sounds were like distant thunder, the squeaking of the rubber soles on the floor, and every so often a half-stifled shout for a bungled or exceptionally good shot. The endless recycling of the same repeated movements came to feel absurd to her, as though the team was made up of robots on an assembly line, producing some substanceless product. Astrid was unable to tear herself away, she watched until the moment the coach kept hold of the ball, clasping it to his chest, as though unwilling ever to surrender it, and called the team to him to discuss the next drill. Suddenly she worried one of them might catch sight of her standing by the window, and she took a step back into the darkness.

Most of the players she knew only fleetingly, having met them at matches or at the annual barbecue the team laid on every summer before the holidays. The players' wives turned up with salads and put them out on a collapsible table. Thomas helped at the grill, and Astrid sat at a table with three couples who seemed to be friends and were sharing village gossip, with loud shouts of laughter. When the others joined her at her table, they had briefly introduced themselves and shaken hands, and after that they more or less ignored her. The children paid flying visits to pick up a handful of chips or hurriedly drink a glass of iced tea. When Astrid asked them what they were playing, they gave some breathless information and scampered away to rejoin the other children. By the time Thomas finally jammed himself onto the bench facing her, laughing at some comment or other that someone had called out, she said she was tired and wanted to go home. She felt like an utter spoilsport, but she had the feeling she couldn't stand the noise and the merriment for another minute. In spite of that, they didn't go home until much later, after midnight, when there was a chill in the air.

Astrid thought of the men going to the bar after practice was finished, and turning up at home half drunk, dropping their sweaty gear on the floor, and creeping into bed beside their sleeping wives.

She walked home. Before she disappeared inside, she hesitated briefly, glanced at the bench, where the newspaper still lay and the half-empty wineglass stood. She left them both outside, as though that were a way of keeping time from moving forward. She didn't turn a light on. She imagined Thomas was already in bed, waiting for her. She slid under the cover next to him. What kept you? he asked with an amused tone, pulled her to him and started kissing her. He put his hand on her breast, let it slide down onto her belly, under her nightie, and between her legs. She thought of him on top of her, could feel his weight and his forceful movements, heard his breathing, his groaning. She came, and then started to cry. She didn't want to sleep, she was afraid of waking up, of another day where Thomas would be even farther from her.

It was almost midday when Thomas awoke. The sky was overcast, the wind had got up. He was cold and felt exposed in his nakedness. Even though his things were still wet, he put them on. It took him a moment to get his bearings, then he walked on by the side of the stream until he came to a narrow valley that headed due south. He followed an asphalt road, climbing steadily, first through trees, then through steep pastureland. The stream was flowing far below in a narrow gully, its distant rushing only feeble now. The smell again was of newly mown grass.

After a while, the valley widened out into a depression, the road divided, went past a group of houses, and was reunited at an isolated cheesery with an adjacent pigsty. The stink of the pigs reminded Thomas of human feces.

At the edge of the wood stood a cross, the ornamental flower bed at the foot of which was like a fresh grave. From a little horsepond, a gray heron flew up with languid wingbeats.

The farmhouses were cladded with wooden shingles, some of them painted in pastel colors. In front of one of them was a little vegetable patch, with beans, fennel, kohlrabi, and beetroot, and tomato vines in an improvised greenhouse of lathes and plastic sheeting. The plastic was rattling away in the stiff gale that was blowing down the slope out of the west. An earthenware pot with a withered hydrangea lay on its side on the ground. Next to the front door, some baby clothes were hanging out to dry, one window was half open but there was no sign of anyone. The entire valley felt abandoned, only once Thomas saw a woman wearing rough work clothes walking across a pasture, apparently looking for something. But before he reached her, she had gotten into an ancient Volvo parked at a passing place and driven off.

A path left the road and led even more steeply up the right side of the valley, past walnut and apple trees. Everything hereabouts looked crooked. There were no straight lines anywhere by which he could orient himself, and he felt mildly giddy. Eventually the path crested a hill, and then led on through pastures with a few dirty cows grazing in them. Everywhere spurge sprouted up in thick bundles. Farther on, where the grass was shorter, he saw the first autumn crocuses. Beside the edge of the pasture was a small cowshed. The ceiling was so low that Thomas was unable to stand upright, and the floor was so dungy that it couldn't have been cleaned for several days. Beside the cowshed was a lean-to, where a couple of bales of hay were stored, along with some tools and fencing materials. He would have been able to hole up here, but he had nothing left to eat and had to go on.

The gale up on the top was even stronger than in the valley. The path seemed to be one that not many people walked; in spots there were only scant marks in the grass to indicate where to go. Cowpats were everywhere, and swarms of large rust-colored flies flew up from them at Thomas's approach.

Finally he reached the highest point. For the first time he was afforded a view of dark wooded hills to the south. In the distance he could make out a section of a lake, and beyond that, in the haze, further chains of hills. As he descended, Thomas had the feeling that something had fallen away from him, a repression, a pain. He stepped out powerfully. At a forest hut, he looked at signposts pointing him in different ways. None of the place-names meant anything to him, so he crossed the woods, still heading south. The terrain grew steeper. Thomas slithered down the incline through neglected second-growth pine and beech that was mostly ineffectual against thorny scrub. Suddenly his foot was in midair, he only just managed to hold on to one of the young saplings. His pulse raced, and he felt a surge of warmth throughout his body. Breathing hard, he pulled himself back up to solid ground. He was angry with himself for being so stupid. The rocks below were not precipitous, but even if he just turned his ankle somewhere, it would be days or even weeks before anyone found him here. Painfully he clambered back, and then crossed the slope at a less steep incline.

Near the bottom of the ravine, he struck a path that went parallel to the crest, and that seemed to be coming from nowhere and going nowhere. A black moth fluttered around his head, and since Thomas didn't have a clue where he was, he just decided to follow it. He thought about fairy tales in which animals helped people who had once been kind to them—tossing a fish back into the sea, kissing a frog, nursing a wounded deer back to health. He himself had always found animals alien, inscrutable, and a little frightening.

In the middle of the wooded slope, surrounded by low scrub, stood a tiny wooden huntsman's shelter. The outside walls had skulls and antlers mounted on them. A rough picnic table and benches had half rotted away, and mushrooms were sprouting from the damp wood. Only a fountain next to the entrance was plashing away merrily to itself and gave the place some feeling of welcome. Thomas drank some water, and then walked on to the bottom of the wooded ravine. The ground became clayey, and the air took on a heavy smell. The narrow footpath that followed the stream downhill was undermined, even completely washed away in places, certainly no one could have walked this way for a long time.

At the end of the valley, the stream flowed into a little river with clear, greenish water. A forest road went alongside the river. Thomas identified north from the shadows of the trees and walked upstream. By and by the gorge narrowed, the sheer cliffs of conglomerate to either side, with their bulbous forms, looked like body parts of enormous fossil creatures. The rocks were full of seams and cracks, a moss-covered sign warned of the danger of rockfalls.

Just before the valley ended in a narrow defile, the road led steeply uphill. Thomas felt shattered. Ever since he had set out, he had eaten little and only napped briefly for hours at a time. His legs were heavy, cold sweat covered his face, and each step was a strain. He had to find a place to stop and rest, but the slope here was too broken. On the top, the woods stopped and a view opened onto a pleasant landscape, green hills, a few farms and villages, and, nearer now, the lake with two small islands in it, and the opposite bank, gently climbing.

From here on, he was going downhill, and Thomas forgot his tiredness, but he kept stumbling as he walked, and, in spite of himself, he was looking for somewhere to rest. The path followed a channel of swiftly moving water, hopping from side to side via numerous little footbridges. For a while Thomas was accompanied by a wagtail that flew beside him step by step, flicking its tail, so close to the surface of the water that it seemed sometimes to brush it. The stream disappeared into a narrow clump of trees; various benches and campfire sites indicated the probable presence of the bank, but none of them was discreet enough for Thomas. Finally he headed into the bushes at an almost level place. With his feet he scraped together some dried leaves, then spread his jacket out over them and lay down.

Normally Astrid found getting up easy, but on this day, after switching off the alarm clock, she went back to sleep and only awoke when Konrad touched her gently on the shoulder and whispered, Mama, are you awake? She put off her shower until later, and groggily got breakfast for herself and the children. Once Konrad and Ella were out of the house, she went back to bed, but sleep wouldn't come, and she tossed and turned restlessly, without managing a clear thought. At nine the telephone rang. Sorry, did I wake you?

asked Thomas's secretary. How is your husband feeling? Do you know when he'll be ready to come back to work? I'm taking him to the doctor this morning, said Astrid, playing for time. I'll call you later on, when I know more.

When she went into the village to do her shopping, and passed the police station, she crossed to the other side and avoided looking at it. Back at home, she rang the police, and asked to speak to Herr Ruf. The woman at the other end asked what it was about. A personal matter, said Astrid. Shortly afterward he was on the line. Astrid asked if he had any news. The moment we hear anything we'll call you, he said. Astrid said nothing. How are you doing? You all right? he asked. No, she said, and laughed hollowly. He apologized. I'm out on patrol all day, but if you like I can look in on you later. Would you, said Astrid. Maybe— But the sentence broke off, and she didn't say any more. See you later then, said the policeman.

At ten, Astrid called the office and said Thomas had shingles. Oh, golly, poor man, said the secretary. My mother had shingles once. Where did he get it from? The doctor says it might have been getting too much sun while on holiday, said Astrid. She had come across the condition online and made notes on it. Do you know how long he'll be off work? Thomas would definitely have to spend the next two weeks at home, said Astrid, and it might be more than a month. It's highly infectious, she added. Well, give him all the best from everyone here, and I hope he's better soon, said the secretary. You can bring in the doctor's note at your convenience. Astrid promised she would, and hung up.

On the coffee table were a few books Thomas had been reading lately, plus a gardening magazine and a brochure for

ecologically approved insecticides. Astrid dumped the catalogue and magazine in the recycling, and put the books
back on the shelf. She picked up Thomas's sweater off the
sofa and dropped it in the washing in the bathroom, and
likewise his pajamas and a pair of socks she found beside the
bed. She took his toiletries off the vanity shelf and packed
them away in the bathroom cupboard. She went through
the house, picking up things he had left lying around, a
half-eaten bag of dried apricots (a present from a client),
a screwdriver, a tube of wood glue, a shopping list, a free-
bie ballpoint. She ate the apricots and tidied everything else
away. In the bedroom was a desk that Thomas sometimes
used. That too she tidied, stuffing loose sheets of paper into
the drawers. In a plastic file folder she found restaurant bills
from their vacation, the rental agreement for the holiday
house, and a few cash withdrawal slips. Finally she wiped the
work surface with a damp cloth, as though to remove every
last trace of Thomas's presence.

Shortly before midday, the doorbell rang. It was Ruf. As
she led the way into the living room, she glanced through
the curtains and saw the patrol car parked beside the garden gate. I've got my colleague waiting for me outside, said
Ruf. For a while they sat facing each other in silence. Finally,
Astrid asked him if he was married. My wife had her first
baby in April, he said. Our first baby. A little girl. You think it
could never happen to you, don't you? said Astrid. He merely
shook his head silently, she couldn't tell whether he was con-
firming or denying her allegation. Then she admitted to him
that she had sometimes left Ella, her older child, all alone
when she was very little. I've never told anyone that, not
even my husband. I think everyone has thoughts like that,

said Ruf. But not everyone acts on them, said Astrid. Thank God. What would you do if you were in my situation? she asked. As I say, most people return within a few days. You should get in touch with everyone he knows, even friends from way back. If he uses his bank or credit cards, you'll see confirmation of it in your records. Other than that, we're relying on Inspector Chance. She could always engage a private detective, but they came dear and wouldn't be able to do much more than the police. It's not so easy to find someone who's set on not being found. You must think I'm a bad wife, said Astrid, why else would he have left me. Tears ran down her face. Ruf hesitated, then took her hand in his, like a small animal he sought to protect or keep from fleeing. No, he said, no, and then with quite unprofessional agitation in his voice, you just don't do something like that. He let go of her hand and stood up. I need to go, my partner's waiting for me outside. Whenever you come here I have to cry, said Astrid.

After midnight Thomas woke up. He had a sense of having been woken by a noise, but he couldn't put his finger on it. He felt reasonably well-rested, only his feet hurt him still.

He walked out of the woods and headed down the slope through the village, first through a residential quarter, then the center, which was traversed by a wide street. Most of the shop windows were still lit, but there was no one around. He had the sense that this village was inhabited predominantly by the objects in the window displays, by kitchen equipment and bicycles, cell phones and fashion items: Everything looked more energetic than the stylized mannequins over whose bodies they were draped.

Now Thomas knew where he was and which way he wanted to go. He was sufficiently far enough away from his house; he felt less shy; he didn't straightaway go into hiding when a car approached, he merely lowered his head and averted his gaze, without slowing his step.

Next door to the station was a snack bar. Inside, an elderly gray-haired woman was just clearing things off the counter and wiping it down. Thomas hesitated, then gave a knock. The woman jumped. She went up to the glass door, gave Thomas a quick once-over, and unlocked the door. We're closed, she said. I'm hungry, said Thomas, his voice sounded cracked, it was two days since he had last spoken to anyone. Do you have any food left over? The woman looked in the glass case behind the counter. There's some börek, she said. Great, said Thomas, you don't need to warm it up. And a beer. Efes okay? asked the woman. She packed them into a white plastic bag and thanked him for the tip. Thomas had spent the last of his money on the meal, but the thought didn't oppress him, on the contrary, he felt freer than before.

The last train had left several hours ago. Thomas sat down on a bench outside the station building and ate and drank the ice-cold beer. As he did so, he leafed through a newspaper that someone had left lying around, but the short news items about the rescue of four stranded sperm whales, a naked statue of Satan that someone had built in Vancouver, and the man with the longest tongue in the world merely depressed him, and he threw the paper into the bin. He took off his shoes and socks and examined his feet in the harsh neon street lighting. They were swollen, and the ankles had abrasions, but luckily he had no blisters.

The village went on seemingly forever. He walked along the road, past a soccer pitch. Opposite was a large factory. There was light behind the closed metal shutters. He could hear the humming of air conditioning, the blades in the opening of the air vent were fluttering gently in the breeze, a sound that somehow reminded Thomas of America. From the conservatory of a crummy restaurant he heard the voices of a couple of drunks, getting worked up about something or other. Next came a sector with new apartment buildings and a bus stop still in the process of construction. The orangey light of the streetlamps made the grass on the shoulders look gray, the crowns of newly planted trees black. Finally the pavement came to an end, and with it the streetlights. Thomas walked on in darkness. Even though there was no moon in the overcast sky, it wasn't completely pitch-black, the clouds gave a pale reflection of the light pollution of civilization. The air was warm and damp.

It was very quiet; no cars had passed for some time. When Thomas crested a hill, he saw in the distance the lights this side of the lake, making a straight line in the expanse of nocturnal landscape. Above it there was a suggestion of mountains, and on the highest peaks the red signal lights used to warn pilots. From time to time a truck went by or a delivery van. A solitary walker on the road was surely more striking at night than by day, but Thomas was obliged to follow the roads; if he had gone cross-country he would have instantly lost his bearings. And to walk through inhabited areas in the daytime, that was something he didn't dare to do.

Once he thought there was a creature padding after him, and he stopped in terror and turned around, but there were no more sounds and nothing to be seen.

The road divided. Almost at random he chose the downhill fork. For about an hour he walked among maize fields and meadows, and past isolated farmhouses. To the regular rhythm of his steps, he started softly singing walking songs that came to him out of his childhood. In our eyes the flashing of starlight and the flames of nightly fires, in our legs the indomitable rhythm and our spirits that never tire.

He passed a small village perched on a slope over the road that seemed to consist entirely of new buildings, identi-kit concrete cubes, surrounded by wire-mesh fences. Lights were on over some of the doorways, but Thomas had difficulty imagining people actually living behind these façades, people lying in their beds, sleeping and dreaming, or waking up in the middle of the night, listening for sounds from the nursery, or thinking of the day ahead or just passed. Over a garage door hung a scarf in the colors of a soccer team, written on it in a spine-chilling font: Welcome to Hell.

Back out in the open again, Thomas heard soft rustling or fluttering sounds, as of dragonflies' wings. Looking around, he saw for the first time the electricity wires that crossed the valley over his head. He walked down the middle of the road, thought he would keep his eyes closed for a hundred paces, and counted them too, but after ninety he couldn't stand the suspense anymore and opened them again.

He was surprised not to have reached the lake long ago. He thought he must be heading in the wrong direction and decided to wait for it to get light and orient himself by the rising sun. He sat down on the shoulder and looked up into the paling sky, where there were barely any stars to be made out.

Finally it got light and Thomas saw that all along he'd been heading westward, parallel to the lake. He took the very next track left, and walked south over a wooded knoll. At the edge of a swampy clearing stood some old oaks, their contorted limbs in the gloaming resembling the outstretched claws of mythical beings. One more rise, and then the silence of the woods suddenly gave way to traffic noise as Thomas found himself standing at a lookout point with a cross and benches, and saw directly in front of him the lake, and off to the right an extensive industrial estate and behind that a town. He had meant to round the lake at its eastern end, but now realized that he was many miles away from his intended route.

The steep slope below was covered with row houses. He got through the area as quickly as he could. Then he walked along past office buildings and apartment blocks toward the lake. He would be better able to hide in the reedy bank during the day than on the wooded hill. In front of a half-dilapidated old apartment building he saw a neglected vegetable patch. In one bed were zucchini plants, probably a dozen enormous yellowed vegetables under white mildewed leaves. Thomas looked around quickly, scrambled over the fence, and picked one. He stuffed it under his jacket and trotted on in the direction of the lake.

On the shore was a campsite. The office was shuttered. There was a note on the door with a cell-phone number to call during office hours. There seemed to be no one around. Most of the trailers seemed to be long lets; they were up on cinder blocks, had awnings, satellite dishes on their roofs, and little front yards with flowers. Thomas had gone in intending to look for somewhere to hide, but when he spotted a rowboat on the edge of the reeds, he decided on impulse to row across the lake. The far side was less built up.

The lake at this point was no more than half a mile wide, but it was tricky to keep the tiny boat on course. Shreds of mist lay over the smooth surface. Even now, in the early morning, the lake seemed to give off a kind of exhaustion, a quality of sloth and heaviness that affected Thomas. When he turned around to check his course, he saw not far from him a motorboat, and a fisherwoman, reeling in her net that was held in the water with a long line of white plastic canisters. Thomas thought about what he would say if she spoke to him. But she didn't pay him any mind, just kept drawing in the net with repetitive motions of her hand, and freed the wriggling fish, while her boat moved on with a quiet put-putting sound.

The rowing was heavy going, and Thomas shivered in the cold that rose from the lake. But even before he could get to the other side, the sun had risen, and he started to get warmer. He had aimed for a wooded point, and only as he approached it did he see that it was in fact the mouth of a little stream. Even at some distance, the current was perceptible, the murky water of the stream mingling gradually with the clear lake water.

He didn't manage to make much headway against the stream, the current was too strong for him. He clambered out on a gravelly bank that was ringed by bushes and trees, and pulled the boat onto the shore. He sat down on a thick, barked tree trunk and with his little pocketknife cut the zucchini in pieces and removed the seeds.

He wouldn't be able to go on like this for much longer, he thought, as he slowly chewed the zucchini pieces. Now, with the mountains ahead of him, he needed better gear, waterproof clothes, and food. He wouldn't find any more snack machines or vegetable beds where he was going, or any dumpsters or dispensers of old bread. He toyed with the idea of stocking up in the nearby village; at least he was far enough from home by now that no one would know him. Also, since he had washed it in the stream, his clothing was sufficiently clean not to attract notice. He consulted his watch. He had at least two hours until the shops opened. He lay down in a sunny spot, stretched out, and closed his eyes. The sun's warmth seemed to flow into him like a substance, filling up the void that the cold had left behind.

Astrid was relieved that the police car was gone before the children came home from school. This time, Konrad arrived almost at the same time as Ella. They were both quiet, but Astrid could feel the pressure of their unasked questions. No one felt at all hungry. What about some ice cream? she asked after clearing away the dirty plates. Ella's thanks were so overwhelming that Astrid was almost reduced to tears again. Come here, both of you, she said. The children approached her with expectant looks. I don't know where Papa is, she said, putting an arm around each of them, nor do I know why he went away, but I'm sure he's doing well, and that he'll come back soon. I didn't tell anyone about it, and I don't want you to talk about it either. All right? It's our business and no one else's. Papa's and ours. The children nodded.

As it was a Wednesday, there was no afternoon school. Astrid asked the children if they had any homework. Usually she had to remind them several times before they did anything, but this time they both settled down at the dining-room table, and quietly and without bickering did what they had to do.

Astrid remembered what Herr Ruf had told her. Without any great hope she turned on the computer and went to the online banking site.

What's the matter? both children exclaimed almost at once. Astrid had gasped with surprise. The latest statement showed three withdrawals since Thomas's disappearance, one a day ago, the other two a matter of hours ago. She clicked on details of the transactions, the two recent ones were done in short order in Lachen on Lake Zurich—one from a cash machine, the other at a sportswear business. For a moment, Astrid sat there stunned, then she said to the children, All right, get a shuffle on, we've got to go. She got out of the drawer the photograph of Thomas that she'd printed out for Herr Ruf, and wrote down the name of the sportswear shop and also the details of the first withdrawal, which was credited to a certain M and K Entertainment in Frauenfeld.

In the car she told the children that their father had used his bank card a few hours ago on Lake Zurich, and that was where they were driving. There wasn't much more to be said, and after they had all been silent for a while, Astrid turned on the radio and straightaway switched it off again because the music was still more insufferable than the silence.

In Zurich there was heavy traffic, even though it wasn't yet the rush hour. Astrid felt increasingly nervous, as though every minute counted. At the end of an hour and a half they were there, and Astrid parked the car in a large gravel area not far from the lake. Ella jumped out, Konrad had fallen asleep. She woke him gently. He stretched and complained a little. Get a move on, said Ella impatiently, otherwise Papa'll have gone again.

They got directions to the sportswear store, which was in a new shopping mall on the edge of town. There was a main nave with high glass ceiling, from where a supermarket and various smaller businesses branched off to the sides. What about waiting for me here? asked Astrid. Ella and Konrad sat on a stone bench outside the sportswear store. Before Astrid went in, she took a last look behind her. Ella was fiddling with her Nintendo, Konrad sat next to her with slumped shoulders, watching. For a moment Astrid was almost overwhelmed with sympathy for them. She herself would somehow manage to deal with Thomas's disappearance, even though she couldn't understand it, but the children were helplessly exposed to their feelings. For years already Astrid had the sense she couldn't get through to them and was merely accompanying them through their lives like some distant observer.

A member of the sales staff asked if she could help. Astrid awkwardly explained what it was about. She held the picture of Thomas in her hand the whole time. The sales assistant hesitated, then said she couldn't give out information about individual purchases. She didn't seem to be terribly sure of her ground. Astrid wondered whether the woman believed a word she, Astrid, was saying, or if she maybe thought she was dealing with a madwoman. Do you think I could speak to the manager? she asked. I wouldn't know anything anyway, said the sales assistant, I only came on shift at noon. Hold on a moment. She disappeared. Astrid looked at the stock: sports gear, sneakers and hiking shoes, camping equipment, freeze-dried MREs. She took a packet in her hand and read through the list of ingredients, as though they would tell her about Thomas's intentions and whereabouts. Then she saw the assistant approaching her again, with a second, younger woman at her side. They were talking, but stopped just before they reached Astrid.

The younger woman shook hands with Astrid and introduced herself: Bordoni, I'm the manager of the store. She had to be more or less Astrid's age, was petite and had a pretty face and long dark hair. Even though her staff member would certainly have told her what it was all about, she asked to hear everything again from the beginning. Astrid named the substantial sum of money that Thomas had spent in the store and the time of the transaction. The assistant had gone away to look after another customer. I'm afraid I'm not allowed to give you any information, said the manager, you see, I can't even check your story. Astrid cast a despairing look out into the mall, but the bench where she had left Ella and Konrad wasn't visible from where she stood. The strength drained out of her, she felt dizzy and grabbed hold of the nearest thing, which happened to be a green down jacket that slid off its hanger and fell to the floor. Astrid found herself gripping the stand, and hung there almost doubled up, and struggling for breath. Do you not feel well? asked the manager. Come with me. She took Astrid under the arm, and walked her to a back room behind the counter with the cash registers. Sit down, I'll bring you a glass of water. She remained standing in front of Astrid while she drank. I've got my children waiting outside, said Astrid, I have to check up on what they're doing. Better now? asked the manager. Astrid nodded. Is that your husband? asked the manager, pointing to the photo that Astrid was still clutching in her hand. Let's see it. She looked at the picture quickly and gave it back. I was the one who served him this morning, but there's not much more I can tell you. For a tiny moment, Astrid had the absurd thought that the woman was on Thomas's side, his secret lover and co-conspirator, and the two of them were playing a hideous trick on her.

Jennifer, said the woman, shaking hands with her again. Her husband had come in soon after the shop had opened, she had asked him if she could help, but he had declined and said he just wanted to have a look around. Then I served another customer, she said. I thought he might have gone already, when he walked up to the checkout counter with a whole pile of merchandise. Can you tell me what he bought? asked Astrid. To give you precise details I'd have to check at the register, but I think I can remember most of it. A pair of hiking shoes, a pair of trekking pants, a waterproof jacket, a rucksack. She stopped to think. A battery torch, no, it was a headlamp. And socks, we've got them on sale. I think that was everything. No, there was a pocketknife as well. I remember I had to unlock the window. One of the new ones from the Pioneer range, with black Alox scales. Did he say anything to you? asked Astrid. What he wanted it for? Where he was going? I made some remark about the weather, said the manager, that it was supposed to rain tonight. But he didn't say much. I don't remember. I see so many customers every day. How did he strike you? asked Astrid. What was his appearance like? His manner? Friendly. He seemed a bit tired possibly, and he was unshaven. His shirt was crumpled. Otherwise nothing. Just an ordinary customer.

Astrid took the children through the city. They walked into every restaurant and looked around, asked after Thomas in the few hotels, but there was no trace of him. In the station was a big hiking map, a dense web of green lines going in every direction, roads and trails, bus and train lines. It was almost ten hours since Thomas had made his purchases, by now he could be anywhere. If she hadn't had the children with her, Astrid might have set off on her own to look. It had started raining gently, as the manager had predicted. The children complained, they were hungry and tired. What would you say to a pizza? asked Astrid. The children were jubilant, as though they had already forgotten what they were here to do.

Thomas had the disquieting feeling that all this had been laid on for him, that the people in the village were actors who were merely waiting for him to come by, to assume their roles and speak their lines. It was an artificial world, a model construction under an expansive blue sky. The sun was shining, the houses gleaming in the morning light. An old lady and an old gentleman, both with dogs, stood by the side of the road talking about the weather; a woman going past on her bicycle called out a greeting to them; schoolchildren were practicing long jumps on the playing field; on the kindergarten playground smaller children were fizzing around. Thomas passed through the village, simultaneously extra and onlooker. Cars crawled past at walking speed, a sales assistant was cleaning the window of a leather goods store, two workmen exchanged banter with her. A young mother leaned over the baby carriage and spoke soothingly to her infant. The words and gestures seemed as exaggerated as those of amateur performers in a village theatrical.

Thomas asked a young man in suit and briefcase if he knew a sports shop, and had him show him the way. The shopping center was on the main road, not far from the station. It seemed not to have been open for very long, some of the premises were still unfinished, which only added to Thomas's sense of moving about on a stage.

After days out of doors, even the lofty mall felt constricting, but Thomas enjoyed the fixed temperature, the bluish neon, and the simple artificial smells of shoes and textiles. Here was a limited world with no surprises and no dangers. A young shop assistant addressed him. He said he was just having a look around. While he gathered up the things he needed, he kept on seeing her. She was filling shelves, giving instructions to a colleague, serving a customer, who seemed to take forever before deciding on a pair of sneakers. The assistant radiated a kind of bustling happiness that suited this unreal place to a tee. As he paid, she asked him with a routine show of interest if he was planning a hike. I thought I'd go to the mountains, said Thomas, and after a brief pause for thought, as though he was reassuring himself, again, yes, the mountains. But the sales assistant was busy removing the security tabs from his purchases and seemed not to be listening. He looked at her hands, which looked older than her conservatively made-up face, the nails carefully manicured and lacquered; she wasn't wearing a ring. Her hands brought him around to her. He felt almost certain that she had no husband, no lover, at the most a cat. He imagined her going home after work to her little apartment in one of the gigantic blocks he had seen at the edge of town. Surely her apartment would be just as tidy as this store, the town, the whole area. She would take a shower, fix herself a salad, keep the radio on while she ate. What would she say if he asked her if she had anything planned for tonight? He thought of finding refuge in her place. While she took her shower, he would be camped in the kitchen listening to the sounds from the bathroom. She would emerge in a kimono, with her hair wrapped up in a towel, take some food out of the fridge, get her dinner ready. He sat there in silence, watching her eat. He sat next to her in front of the TV, and later, when she went to bed, he of course slipped in under the sheets beside her. While she was at work the next day, he would be in the apartment waiting for her to come home. Until one day he moved on, now a long way from home in time as well as distance. Cash or credit, she asked. Credit, said Thomas.

At a cash machine he withdrew a thousand francs. In the supermarket next to the sports store he bought a large bottle of water and as much food as he could fit into his rucksack, things that were nutritious and would keep: biscuits and chocolate, salami, hard cheese, rye bread in slices, dried fruit and nuts, and—after a moment's hesitation—a small bottle of inexpensive brandy. Then he went to the shopping center's restroom and got changed. He dumped his old stuff in a trash can.

Thomas felt happy to be leaving the town. Ideally, he would have been walking out at night, but he hadn't been able to find a place to spend the day unobserved. At least he looked like a legitimate hiker now, suitably dressed, with heavy boots and a rucksack. But his new equipment weighed him down, and he made slower headway than previously. He followed the yellow footpath signs under the motorway and then across the flatland to the next place, a farming village, at whose edges dozens of new buildings stood among barns and cow pastures. These buildings looked as though they had fallen from the sky, an enemy invasion from more urban zones. Ahead he saw a slightly elevated col and far at the back jagged rocks, but the footpath followed a little road that zigzagged up the side of the slope. The higher Thomas climbed, the more he saw of the densely settled flatland below. Ringed by mountain chains it had the appearance of a gigantic arena. In the distance he could see the lake, and beyond it a further array of villages, woods, and hills, the autobahn and the railway line. Again, he was put in mind of a scale model, a papier-mâché landscape, sprinkled with artificial green and dotted about with little houses and trees from catalogues.

Only right at the top did the trail lead into the valley, and along the western slope into the south. Isolated farmhouses were dotted about. From a wooded area below the road rose a column of smoke. On the opposite side thick high-pressure pipes led down to the hydraulic power plant on the plain. His road was now gently downhill, meeting the rising valley. After a couple of miles of easy walking, Thomas reached the valley floor. The landscape spread out and the wooded slopes gave way to green meadows with grazing sheep and cows on them. A substantial village followed, with a self-service gas station and a closed grocery store. At the upper edge of the village was a campsite that was stuffed full of old caravans. A few had improvised roofs of corrugated PVC or plastic sheeting. Outside one of them sat an old man and a little girl, both impassive, as though under a spell.

Soon after, the valley narrowed into a wooded gorge. The trail led along a streambed where some huge rocks lay, but no water. A signpost warned of the risks of flash floods, even in fine weather. Through the treetops Thomas glimpsed the crest of a dam. A narrow path led up the side of the slope and then zigzagged up a cliff. Some spots had been fitted with handholds and wire balustrades.

When Thomas emerged from the woods, he felt he had arrived in a different world. He was standing at one end of the dam, ahead of him lay the man-made lake, edged with woods and meadows. On the other side of the reservoir was a small village. The rough gray peaks on the horizon seemed to loom over him, very near. Cirrus clouds hung there, while Thomas still had blue sky overhead. He walked along the edge of the reservoir, then sat down in the grass to eat and rest. He heard a distant clanging of cowbells. He lay down and was soon in a sort of half sleep, where places and times blurred into a blissful feeling of endlessness.

No sooner had Astrid set off than the children were asleep, even though it was only a little after nine. She was relieved not to have to speak to them. Dinner had been laconic enough. The children had shared a pizza, and then Astrid bought them ice creams as though it was a holiday. She didn't manage to finish the salad she had ordered.

She chose the route over the lake and the Oberland, so as not to have to negotiate the city a second time. There was a light drizzle still, and the headlights of the oncoming traffic made gleaming reflections on the wet asphalt. Astrid found the drive in the dark demanding. She'd had little sleep over the past few nights and was afraid of dropping off. She tried to be furious with Thomas, who was to blame for everything, but she didn't manage it. If anything, she was worried about him. She sat bolt upright in her seat, sang quietly to herself, but her exhaustion was like a poison slowly seeping through her body and isolating it against other influences.

She stopped at the service station outside Winterthur and parked beside the little store. She went inside to get a coffee and stood under the awning, from where she could keep an eye on the children in the car. The hissing of the passing traffic, the reflections of the lights on the wet surfaces, the smell of petrol all reminded her of long drives on Sunday evenings following visits with her parents, and that settled her a little. The coffee was so hot that she had to drink it in tiny sips. Only now did it occur to her to phone the police to tell them about the latest turn of events. She took Herr Ruf's card out of her purse and looked at her watch. It was ten o'clock. Hesitating briefly, she punched the mobile number he had written on the back. There were half a dozen rings before he answered. Am I bothering you? she asked. No problem, he said. I normally go to bed pretty late. She could hear a baby crying in the background. More than ever just lately, he said with a dry laugh. I was just changing her ... Astrid didn't want to know. She interrupted him, and talked about the three recent transactions on the account, and that she had been to the sportswear store. Well, that all sounds pretty encouraging, said Herr Ruf. Where are you now? At the service station outside Winterthur. The policeman hesitated. We could have a K-9 detail put on him. What's that? A sniffer dog. Go home and call me again when you're back. By then I should know more.

Astrid felt quite alert now. All at once Thomas seemed to be very close to her, but at the same time she dreaded the moment when he would be facing her and trying to explain his actions. It was as though their relationship had been frozen at the moment three days ago when she went into the house to settle Konrad. As long as Thomas stayed away, nothing would change. Only with his return would time begin to tick on again. And then everything could happen.

She parked the car in front of the house and woke the children. It took a long time before they had finally cleaned their teeth and were in their beds. A little before eleven, Herr Ruf called back. He said he would come by in fifteen minutes.

Astrid waited for him outside the door; she didn't want him to ring and wake the children. She had brewed fresh coffee, and when she sat opposite the policeman at the living-room table, she felt a kind of satisfaction that he had left his wife and baby in the middle of the night to come and help her. There were more important things to do here. He said he had spoken to colleagues in the canton of Schwyz who had a sniffer dog, only it was based in the city. I've offered them one of our dog handlers, that'll be quicker. We'll drive off first thing tomorrow. The track will still be fresh. If the terrain turns out to be difficult, I'd rather not be out at night.

But only yesterday, you were saying you couldn't help me, said Astrid. You said that Thomas had the right to disappear if he wanted to. Yes, he has such a right, said Herr Ruf, but we have a right to look for him. Still, he's been gone for three days and three nights. He said every missing person case was different, there were no standard procedures, just gut instinct. And what does your gut instinct tell you? asked Astrid. I'm afraid that's exactly what my boss will ask me tomorrow morning, said Herr Ruf. But that shouldn't be your concern. The main thing is finding your husband. Now, do you have an item of his clothing? Preferably underclothing, something that will have only his scent on it. I put all his things in the wash, said Astrid. I don't know why. She propped her head in her hands and started to cry. The policeman came around the table, put his hand on her shoulder, and said calmly, There, there, we'll find something, a jacket, a sweater, something.

Once Astrid had calmed down, she went on ahead to the bedroom and opened the wardrobe. Despondently she stared into it. What about that sweater? asked Herr Ruf. He hasn't worn that one for years. She looked at all the freshly laundered things, the pressed shirts, the carefully folded T-shirts he had worn on their vacation. Finally, she remembered Thomas's handball things. In the sports bag on the basement steps they found a pair of tracksuit bottoms. Don't touch them, said Herr Ruf, and he secured the item.

They went back down to the living room and drank a second cup of coffee each. At some point Astrid said, I think I need a brandy now. I expect you're not allowed to drink when you're on duty? That's what the detectives always say on TV. The policeman motioned he wasn't strictly speaking on duty, and he wasn't a detective either. When they knocked glasses, he said, the name's Patrick. They chatted for a while. He started telling her about his baby again. All of Astrid's knowledge of the police came from TV shows. The policemen in those were always in broken relationships or lived apart from their wives, which seemed more appropriate to her than Patrick's little domestic bliss. He refused a second brandy. She poured one for herself and felt much more mature and experienced than him. Even his indignation over Thomas's disappearance struck her as naïve now, and she doubted whether he would be able to achieve anything in a case whose basics he didn't grasp properly. After that she felt better disposed to him, and admitted that she didn't understand what had happened any more than he did. Eventually the baby will sleep through, she said, getting up, it's just some learn faster than others.

Do you know anything about the first withdrawal from the account? Patrick asked as they were already standing in the corridor. Some M and K Entertainment in Frauenfeld, said Astrid. I thought it might be a bar or restaurant. And how high was the sum? Twenty francs, she said. One moment, he said, I'm just going to make a call. He went outside, closing the door behind him. Astrid remained in the corridor. She looked at the time, it was already after midnight. A few minutes later, Patrick came back in. He seemed tired, it was as though something had robbed him of all his energy while he was outside. I'm sorry, he said, but there was something about the name of that company. It seemed familiar. Unfortunately it keeps cropping up in our records. The withdrawal must have been made in the Galaxy, which is a club in a place called Braunau near Wil. Astrid looked at him uncomprehendingly. A brothel, he said. She turned and ran into the living room. All she wanted was to be alone, not see anyone and have no one see her. But Patrick had come after her. Again, he laid his hand on her shoulder. She gave an angry twitch, and he took it away. I'm sorry. It's only a small sum. Presumably all he did was have a beer. Astrid did not say anything. Well, I'll be on my way, he said. Tomorrow will be a long day. I'll keep you informed.

Astrid heard the front door close behind him. She filled Patrick's glass. As she drank, she had the feeling of their lips touching. Then she carried the coffee things and the brandy snifters into the kitchen. She wondered if Thomas had been to that brothel earlier, whether he had possibly been deceiving her all along. He had clients in the area whom he visited from time to time, admittedly in the daytime, but places like that were surely not only open at night. She opened up the laptop and googled the place. A photograph of a bare-breasted woman popped up on the screen, and under the name of the bar, a flashing slogan: The Hottest Club in Eastern Switzerland. Hot, private girls, drinks at bar prices. Open seven days a week, 6:00 p.m. to 5:00 a.m.

She navigated her way through the site, found pictures of the rooms and a gallery of the prostitutes. These girls await your pleasure tonight: Milena, Brigitta, Amanda, Lora, Tina, Maria. Attached were pictures of women in their underwear or entirely naked. Some had their hair falling into their faces, others had yellow stars covering their faces and pudenda. When she clicked on the picture, a new page opened with a brief description of the woman and some more pictures. Insatiable, no limits, sex-addicted. This hot-blooded chick needs sex the way she needs air to breathe. She'll show you desire and submission that you won't get at home. Disgustedly, Astrid closed the browser and snapped the laptop shut.

It took her a long time to get to sleep. Again and again she saw the pictures of the anonymous women with their fantasy names, turning their bottoms to the camera, arching their backs to make their breasts appear bigger and firmer. Astrid saw herself walking into the nightclub in her nightie, with couples along the walls and little groups of masked men and women all naked. She sensed that these people knew her and saw through her. They came closer and ever closer, surrounded her. Astrid tried to get away, but they wouldn't let her through; she felt hands pushing her back, plucking at her nightie, her underthings, arms wrapping themselves around her and holding her fast. Then through the crowd she saw Thomas standing by the wall. He had his arm draped over the hip of a naked woman and there was an amused smile on his face. His lips were moving, but with all the noise she couldn't make out what he was saying. Suddenly she was wide awake. It was dark in the room. She groped for the alarm clock. It was four in the morning. She got up, threw on her dressing gown, and went out into the garden. And then she could breathe again.

The sun was over the other side of the valley, and the clouds had come nearer, otherwise everything was the same as before. Thomas thought about the paired images he had seen in his childhood, how many differences can you find. A cow was gone, one of the many flowers in the meadow had lost all its petals, the blackbird was no longer in the apple tree, the white cross had quit the Swiss flag. There was a fishing boat out on the lake, but the fisherman must be around the other side of the boat or in the cabin.

The road followed the lakeshore. The occasional angler sat, as motionless and quiet as though he belonged to the landscape. Otherwise there was no one in sight. Over everything hung a festive atmosphere. The sun was dazzling. Then there was a bend in the road, and he was walking through the blue shadows of a little alder wood. The trunks were scurfy and dabbed with moss, which didn't seem to go with their luminous leaves. On the meadows he saw more autumn crocuses, which looked somehow feebler than flowers in spring, anxious, as though they could sense the shorter days ahead.

At the end of the lake was an area of buoys with a few small motorboats; on the shore were some vacation houses with lowered blinds and a restaurant. Open Today, it said on a sign over a drinks advertisement, and the glass door was open wide, but the terrace was empty.

The gravel track now turned through a wood up a steeply climbing valley. On either side of the path were enormous mossy boulders. Thomas had a stitch that wouldn't go away, even though he kept stopping to get his breath back. The road ended at a half-wrecked croft, which had evidently not been in use for a long time. Even though it was early in the day, he decided to spend the night here. He didn't know the area, and he was afraid that it might get cold higher up.

Above the former cowshed was a hayloft, where he made up a bed for himself. He spread the dusty leftover hay over the plank flooring and laid his dark green rain jacket over it. Then he emptied his rucksack and spread all his things out on the thin PVC. He felt like a child who had seen his presents on the eve of his birthday, satisfied but also a little disappointed, even at the fulfillment of all his wishes. It was the embarrassment of the possessor, who realizes that no object could satisfy or still his desires. He took out his penknife, opened and shut all the blades and tools, and attached it on a spring hook to the chain he had bought to carry it. Then he took out the calendar he had found in the jacket he had taken in the nightclub. He flicked through the pages reading the entries, names and times, a doctor's appointment, a hairdresser's. The name of one woman kept turning up, Brigitta. Thomas didn't know any Brigitta, but even so she sounded familiar. He pictured a slightly older woman, not especially attractive but serious and good-hearted. He wondered about her relationship with the owner of the calendar, whether she guessed that he visited brothels, and what she would say if she knew. He thought of Milena from Romania, who was so utterly different from the way he had imagined prostitutes.

Thomas shooed away these thoughts. He read the calorie tables on the packaging of the food he had bought, and on an empty page of the calendar wrote them down and totted them up. If he kept his intake down, his food would last him for two weeks, though admittedly it would be a very monotonous diet. He should have bought some fresh fruit, or at the very least some vitamin pills. Even while he was still calculating, it began to rain. He heard the steady rustling sound and felt the cold that came with it. In one or two places it was coming through the old slate roof. He didn't dare to make a fire and ate just a little of the food from his rucksack. Then he had to go out once briefly to fill his canteen at the stream. He came back to his hayloft shivering and wet. He took a swallow from the brandy bottle and lay down. The sound of the rain was soothing, the smell of old hay and grass and wet stone. He thought of Astrid and the children, no concrete memories or thoughts, not even scenes, just a vague feeling of their association: that warmed him.

It was their fourth breakfast without Thomas there. The children seemed to have adjusted to the new situation, asking no questions and seeming somehow less cowed than on the past few days. They even started to bicker again, which Astrid took to be a positive sign. She was feeling better too, not from habituation but because she knew that today the police would go looking for Thomas, and that they had every

chance of finding him. The rain shouldn't really be a problem, Patrick had told her last night; the dog could pick up a
scent regardless, especially a fresh scent. She had given him
her mobile number and asked him to keep her up-to-date.

All morning she got little bulletins from Patrick. We're
on the way, the dog has picked up the scent, we've found
some old clothes we think are his. We're in the Wägi valley.
To distract herself, Astrid busied herself by making an album
of the nicest holiday pictures, as in other years. The photo
software offered various presentational ideas, and Astrid
tried out a few, but the illusion of customizing only made
the photographs themselves more anonymous. She ended up
by choosing a neutral white background and arranged them
as she had done previously with her albums, when she had
still stuck down the photos by hand. She and Thomas took
turns with the camera, and she was in some of the pictures,
sometimes with the children, sometimes on her own. She,
though, had only taken pictures of the kids, the landscape,
a few highlights from Barcelona, where they had gone on
a day trip. So that Thomas should appear at least once in
the album, she put in the picture she had sent the police,
even though it looked nothing like the others and stuck out
among the holiday shots.

Patrick's last text message from the Wägi had come just
before eleven. It was a long time until his next communica-
tion. Astrid had cooked lunch, the children had come home,
they had eaten together, and Ella and Konrad had gone back to
school. Gradually Astrid began to feel uneasy and was beginning to wonder whether she should call Patrick, when at two
o'clock her cell phone rang. Patrick said they had followed
the scent right up the Wägi to the dam and along the side of

the reservoir, they had walked more than twelve miles. Now they were in an abandoned upland farm above the lake, where Thomas had presumably spent the night. Only the dog was exhausted and unable to go on. Twenty kilometers was a huge distance even for a highly trained animal. Isn't there another dog you could use? asked Astrid. Or couldn't he rest, and then carry on? There was a brief silence, then Patrick said his boss said they had invested enough time and trouble in this case. There was no serious suggestion that the missing man was in any danger. On the contrary. Astrid said nothing, and after a further pause Patrick said there weren't that many trails that led on from there. He could have got across into the Klön valley, but that would mean backtracking for a long way, which he wouldn't want to do. The likeliest thing is that he walked over the Pragel Pass into the Muota valley. If he set off this morning, he could already be there. He said he had alerted his colleagues in Schwyz Canton to the ongoing search, and that was about all he could do. So what happens now? Astrid asked finally. We're heading back, said Patrick, sounding bashful. Astrid cut the line without thanking him or saying goodbye.

She left the phone on the dining-room table, went up to the bedroom, and lay down on the bed. It was as though the conversation had taken time to have its full effect, like a medication that first had to be absorbed into the bloodstream and then distributed throughout the body. After she had lain there perfectly still for a quarter of an hour, she finally started to cry violently and uncontrollably. Even when she heard the front door and Ella's surly hello, she couldn't stop. Mama, where are you? called Ella. Shortly afterward she came to the bedroom. Astrid turned away from her onto her front, and, still crying, buried her face in the pillow.

She must have fallen asleep like that. When she woke up, Ella was standing in the doorway, with the policeman next to her and Konrad behind them. The children were talking softly to her: Mama, are you awake? Mama, what's the matter? How are you feeling? Ella touched her. Konrad lay down on the bed and pressed himself against her. His small, warm body. But Astrid couldn't stand to be touched; she turned away again and didn't say a word. Come on, kids, she heard Patrick saying quietly, and then footsteps, and then later Patrick's calming voice and the voices of the children from the living room. The light in the room was beginning to go when she got up. Without turning on the light, she stopped and listened by the open bedroom door. A childhood memory of being ill and delirious, somewhere between sleeping and waking. The TV was going, the wacky voices of cartoon figures. She sneaked into the bathroom and washed her face in cold water. Then she went back to bed.

There was a ring at the door. The bedroom was almost completely dark, what little light there was came from the streetlamp outside. Astrid heard the cheerful voice of Manuela in the hall, and the glee of the children, because each of the few times she came to see them, she brought useless presents. How Patrick could have presumed to call Thomas's sister, with whom Astrid had never gotten along. Presumably her name was the only one that occurred to the kids. Who could look after them and mind their mother? Didn't she have any girlfriends? Any relations? Someone who lived locally, if possible?

There was a knock on the bedroom door. Patrick came in and stood sheepishly next to Astrid's bed. I need to go now, he said, but your sister-in-law's come. She said she could stay the night and look after you and the children until you're feeling better. He said he was sorry they hadn't managed to find Thomas. Astrid shook her head and thanked him for his help. Don't tell her I'm still awake, she whispered. I just told her the bare minimum, he said. He stood there a moment longer, and then went away.

Later on, Astrid could hear the voices of Manuela and the children. All of them seemed to be making an effort to keep it down. Astrid heard steps on the stairs, the toilet flush, a softly sung lullaby, then laughing and whispering and another round of steps on the stairs. She shut her eyes. Just after, she sensed the door opening and shutting—it happened in complete silence, but she could feel the change in the space, which seemed to expand and then contract again.

For the first time since Thomas had set off, he woke rested and full of pep. The rain had stopped, but the sun hadn't yet peeped around the tall mountain sides, and the air felt damp and cold. In the morning light, the clear gray and green planes of the landscape looked almost painted. After breakfasting on bread and dried fruit, Thomas packed his things and set off. The path was even steeper now than it had been the day before, and Thomas soon lapsed into the slow swaying gait he had gotten used to in the mountains and could keep up for hour after hour. The wood came to an end and vegetation grew scarcer. The meadows were full of thistles, the edge of the path was sown with rampion and snow gentians, and tiny ferns sprouted from splits in the rock. All the way he could hear the rushing of the stream, but once the path turned past a big boulder, it was suddenly perfectly quiet. Thomas could hear nothing but the scraping of his soles on the gravelly ground and his breathing, which had adapted to his stride pattern. He felt suddenly present as never before; it was as though he had no past and no future. There was only this day and this path on which he was slowly making his way up the mountain. Once, a marmot whistled, and Thomas stopped and scanned the mountainside like a huntsman, but he could see no sign of the animal.

On reaching the level of the pass, he sat down on a rock and took off his shoes and socks to rub his feet a little. He had sweated during the climb, now he froze in the cold wind and pulled on his jacket, which he had worn tied around his waist. He ate bread and dried beef and a few squares of chocolate.

Ahead of him, the land fell away in a wide valley, pointing first south then curving to the west. Beyond loomed a massive dome of rock, a flat ridge that looked utterly ill at ease among the snowy peaks and bare as though it came from another world. In the sunlight splitting the clouds the formation took on a silvery glitter, almost white, which intensified his sense that heaven was closer than earth. Thomas felt a strange excitement as he set off.

He had to go down a long way and lost a lot of altitude. Grazing cattle had left deep holes in the claggy soil, which had filled with water, a tangle of seeming paths that led nowhere. To Thomas's right the valley was edged by a long line of rock, the grass under the cliff face was littered with scree, and from time to time he could hear the dry clack of a falling stone.

Thomas had seen the highland croft from a long way off. On the pastures around the hut and shed there were goats grazing, a few horses, and a couple of donkeys. As he got closer, he saw an old woman, who was sitting on a wooden bench on a knoll, looking across at the silvery rock formation with a telescope. He was afraid he might give her a start, so he hailed her from a long way off, but she reacted perfectly calmly, as though she had spotted him long ago and was only waiting for him to get there. She set down the telescope on the bench at her side, and with a friendly voice returned his greeting. He asked her about the rock. Our summer grazing is over there. Is there even grass up there? asked Thomas. The old woman nodded. Yes, behind the rock. But the karst is full of holes and splits. They were now both looking over at the gray rock. Almost every year a sheep or cow falls to its death, said the woman. This summer we've been lucky so far, with no accidents. And please God it'll stay that way. She said her family were on their way down from the alp tomorrow. They had originally meant to stay a week longer, but the forecast was for snow. They talked about the rainy summer and that the local weatherman had predicted a cold winter. The content of the conversation seemed not really to be the point, it was just about breaking the silence in this solitary landscape. Finally, Thomas took his leave. The old woman thanked him, he didn't know what for, and picked up her telescope again.

Before long, a narrow pass road appeared below Thomas that wound its way up the mountain. It was a single-lane road, but every few minutes a sports car would come roaring up, sometimes whole convoys of vehicles. The wailing of the over-gunned motors tore the silence; the noise came and went as the cars zipped around one corner and disappeared around the next.

There was a small chapel at the pass and in front of it a tall flagpole with a Swiss flag. The other side of a flat meadow Thomas saw a few buildings, a longish cow barn, and a dwelling house. Presumably there was an inn there as well, maybe even somewhere to stay the night, at any rate there were a few cars parked. It was late afternoon, the sky had clouded over, and it felt chilly, so he decided he would stay the night here.

Astrid woke up early and was unable to get back to sleep. The confusion of the previous night seemed covered over by a great clarity. Her forces seemed to all be pulling together, as if under a great threat. She knew what had to be done, without needing to think about it. She didn't care about Thomas's plans or objectives. Whatever he'd had in mind, she wasn't about to let him go unopposed. She would bring him back. What was on the agenda now was just putting her plan into effect. When she heard Manuela and the kids getting up, she pretended to be asleep again. After the children had left the house, she got up. Manuela was just tidying up in the kitchen. When Astrid walked in, her sister-in-law silently hugged her, as though they were meeting at a funeral. Impatiently, Astrid endured the hug. I'm so sorry, said Manuela, once she'd finally let go of her. These things happen, Astrid said coolly. Manuela poured two cups of coffee and led the way into the living room. She was behaving as though it was her house, as though she was the host and Astrid had come around for a chat. On the sofa lay a woolen blanket, where Manuela had apparently been curled up.

It's so unusual for Thomas, she said. I can't imagine what got into him. Thank you for minding the kids, said Astrid.

But of course, said Manuela, that's what kinship is for. You're not kin, thought Astrid. We're pretty sure we know where Thomas is, she said. We, she thought, Patrick and I. The idea that Manuela might have talked to him about her upset her. It felt as though he had betrayed her. I want to drive to the Muota valley, it's possible someone has seen him there. You can't trust the police to do anything. Could you look after the kids just today? Manuela put on a long-suffering expression. Do you really think that's a good idea? she asked, as though talking to an invalid. I feel perfectly fine, said Astrid. It's the one lead we have. Maybe…she trailed off. You mustn't imagine I'm on his side, just because I'm his sister, said Manuela, I think what he did is so out of character. Out of character is interesting, thought Astrid, that just means he would never do such a thing, it's not in him, and it's your fault for driving him away. She asked herself whether Manuela might know anything about Thomas's whereabouts. The two siblings had always had a certain closeness which she had never understood, and which irked her. She herself had grown up as an only child, and couldn't imagine what it was like to have a brother or sister. Of course Manuela was on Thomas's side, even if she denied it. It drives me crazy to be sitting around when I know where he is, said Astrid. Did you have a fight? asked Manuela, still in her therapist's voice. If you won't look after the kids, I'll ask the neighbor, said Astrid.

It was after nine o'clock before she was on the road. Her GPS informed her that the drive to the Muota valley would take two hours. Astrid drove the speed limit; shortly before eleven she left the autobahn. The country road took her uphill, and soon she was in a flat upland valley. Right at the end of the valley was the village, which seemed to consist of a single long street. She left the car outside a restaurant, took the picture of Thomas out of her bag, and got out. What immediately struck her was the quiet that lay over the valley. All sounds seemed somehow muffled, and the people she asked about Thomas answered so quietly and hesitantly it was as though they were part of a crowd that happened to have witnessed some great spectacle and didn't want to draw attention to themselves. Without the children and in this unfamiliar setting she found it easier to inquire after Thomas. Have you seen this man? He must have been through here last night? He was wearing hiking clothes. Probably unshaven. But even as she asked the handful of passersby, she sensed that Thomas hadn't been through here. He would have tried to avoid the village and stick to the slopes on the opposite side where it was mostly cow pastures, with just the occasional farm and stall. The people were not unfriendly, but they were tight-lipped and unforthcoming, a few just shook their heads and walked on. A couple of schoolkids who spilled laughing out of the bus and then straightaway fell silent, as though their merriment was out of place here, asked if the man had committed a crime. Astrid had come up with a story, an explanation, but now, when put to it, she just said no, he's my husband. The schoolchildren hadn't seen Thomas either.

Astrid wasn't at all hungry, but she went into the restaurant where she had parked her car. The room was empty except for the landlady sitting at one of the tables, watching a rerun of a talk show on television. When Astrid came in, she switched off the television and turned on the radio. A brass band played a medley of familiar pop tunes. By and by the tables filled with workmen and laborers in orange work clothes. Apart from the landlady, Astrid was the only woman in the place. She ordered the special, but the sight of the brimming plate took away her appetite, and she pecked around, eating barely half of it. When the landlady took her plate, she asked if she hadn't enjoyed her meal.

Most of the men were on to their coffee by now. Astrid went from table to table, asking about Thomas. Over their food, the workers had been joking and laughing and Astrid was worried they would make fun of her and her questions, but it was as though the men sensed the seriousness and urgency of the matter, and they answered politely and without any inappropriate remarks. You should ask the guys over there, said a young man, whose dark blue fleece was covered with sawdust, pointing to a group in orange overalls, they're from the building site on the main road. The road workers were no less friendly. A small fat man with a bushy beard, presumably their foreman, looked at the picture for a long time before shaking his head and passing it on to a colleague. Have any of you seen him? The landlady had stepped up to the table and looked at the picture over the shoulder of one of the road workers. Is there a hotel in the village? asked Astrid. The Post restaurant has a couple of rooms for guests, said the landlady. And up in Stalden there's the Alpenblick, and a dormitory in the pass. The radio was playing a popular hit.

After drawing a similar blank at the Post and the Alpenblick, Astrid decided to drive up to the pass. The road was single-lane — it was lucky there were a number of passing places. Astrid was perplexed by the many sports cars coming the other way. Most of them had German plates. She had cracked open the window, and cold, fresh mountain air was coming in.

Fairly near the top, two bearded cowherds were coming down the road with twenty head of cattle, and she was forced to reverse back to the last passing place. The animals trotted past her with loudly clanging cowbells, and the men acknowledged her with a silent nod that had something surly about it. Astrid thought it was early for them to be going down the mountain, then she remembered the forecast had been for snow above six thousand feet.

At the pass, there was a croft with attached café and store. Behind the plain buildings in a fenced-in pasture stood about a hundred cattle, along with a few men and women who were separating them in different groups. The scene had nothing of the joyousness of the Alpine descents with which Astrid was familiar from tourist brochures and cheese commercials; there were no colorful costumes or flower-decked cows, just two heavily laden horses grazing at the edge of the pasture and a small herd of goats.

Astrid parked on the gravel. She was wearing a sweater, but she still felt cold. Dark clouds were massing in the sky, and she could almost smell the coming snow.

Only two of the tables were occupied in the large room. There was a couple at one, a man and a woman of Astrid's age, both in biker gear and with their helmets on the table, and at the other there were four people playing cards, locals, to go by their dialect. A girl was serving at the bar, terribly shy, giving monosyllabic replies to Astrid's questions, before finally saying she'd go and get her mother. It felt like much later when a wiry compact woman with black hair emerged. She was wearing rough work clothes and rubber boots. First she looked at the picture of Thomas, then at Astrid. Finally she said, Yes, the man spent the night here, and left in the morning. We have a little dormitory room under the eaves. Is he your husband? she asked. Come with me. She took Astrid to a table away from the other guests, and called to her daughter to bring two cups of coffee and to let her father know she'd be coming soon. I was just on my way to the cowshed, she said apologetically to Astrid. Now tell me about it. My name's Bernadette. Astrid told her the whole story—she couldn't say why. The farmer's wife listened patiently, asked a couple of questions, and gave from time to time a word or two of comfort. When Astrid was finished, Bernadette had neither comment nor advice for her. She just put her hand on Astrid's forearm and asked if she wanted more coffee. Then she told her what little there was to tell. Astrid's husband had come in late yesterday afternoon and had asked about the possibility of staying the night. She had put him up in the dorm room, he was the only occupant. He had eaten his dinner here, but not said much. Astrid asked how Thomas seemed to her. Bernadette thought for a moment. Friendly, she said, quiet. A bit distant. No, he hadn't said where he was going, she said, but if he came up the Wägi, then he was sure to be headed for the Muota valley, that was a popular hike. No one's seen him there, said Astrid. Of course there's other ways he could have taken, said the farmer's wife. She couldn't remember what time Thomas had set out. He had breakfasted late and paid up. Then she had driven down into the valley to shop, and when she came back at noon or thenabouts, and looked up in the dorm, he was gone. She asked if there was anything else she could do for Astrid. She had to go and milk the cows now.

Astrid walked across the flat upland plain. There were only half as many cows now on the pasture as there had been a moment ago. Where the gradient started to pick up, there was a small open chapel. Astrid spent a long time looking at Christ on the Cross. Her grandmother would have prayed for help; her mother would have crossed herself and had some vague feeling that help was at hand in her extremity. For Astrid it was just a piece of wood and metal.

Down on the road, there were the usual yellow signposts pointing in all directions. Astrid read off the names of the places: Bödmeren, Twärenen, Eigeliswald, Vorauen, Charental, Silberen, Dräckloch. There were dozens of paths Thomas could have taken. Briefly she thought about setting off somewhere at random, just so as not to stand around helplessly anymore. But it was almost four o'clock and about to snow. She could feel the energy that had fired her on from the moment she had gotten up now draining out of her.

The public room was empty when Thomas walked in. Next to the bar was a glass case with Alpine cheese and other milk products. He cleared his throat and sat down at a table to wait. Finally, a rather short, slim woman with black hair walked in, greeted him, and approached his table. There was something Slavic about her, and Thomas thought about the Russian troops who had been this way a couple of hundred years ago. He ordered coffee. When the woman brought it to him, he asked about a room. All they had was the dormitory room, she said, but he was the only guest so far. Dinner was at seven. Thomas watched her as she walked back to the bar and disappeared through the door at the back. She might have been wearing rubber boots, but she moved with a grace that seemed out of keeping with a place like this.

He sipped his coffee and browsed in the local paper that was lying on the table. A while later, the woman came back and said she could show him the lodgings now. She led him past the kitchen and up a narrow set of steps to the attic. In the low, gabled space there were about a dozen narrow mattresses laid out on the floor, with folded gray army blankets on them and pillows in red-and-white-checked slips. A little daylight came in through a narrow window at the front. A single low-watt electric bulb hung over the door. It was cool up here, and there was a clean sour smell of milk and dust and hay. The landlady said again that dinner was at seven and went down. Thomas made up a bed for himself on the mattress under the window. It was just after six, and he lay down and listened to the sounds coming up from downstairs. Shortly before seven he could hear the clatter of silverware, and he went downstairs.

In the public room a long table had been set for ten people, and a little way off, a table for one. Thomas sat down there and watched as the big table filled. The farmer and four children were joined by a young man and an old man, while the farmer's wife and a plump young woman did the serving. The young woman brought Thomas his dinner and wished him a good appetite. He was starving and began to eat right away, while the group at the long table joined hands and the farmer spoke a blessing so quietly it was as though he felt ashamed in the presence of the unknown guest. For a while after that, nothing could be heard but the scrape and clatter of knives and forks. Only gradually voices joined in the sounds of eating, someone asking for a dish or the tea, the young man made a joke, the plump girl retorted, the farmer's wife intervened. Thomas could barely understand half of what was being said, but for the first time since he had set off, he felt lonely. All the time he was walking, he felt oblivious of himself, and whenever he thought of Astrid and the kids, he was with them. Now he had the painful sensation of no longer belonging to a community, that he was a stranger in this small, familiar world. One setting at the long table had remained free, and he imagined what would have happened had he sat there, and held hands with his neighbors, and said grace with them, and ate and drank and later helped clear the table and do the washing up. In an upland farm an extra pair of hands was always welcome.

Flies buzzed around his table, and irritably he kept having to shoo them away. No sooner had he put down his silverware than three of them alighted on his empty plate. He had ordered a half liter of red. He could feel the alcohol take effect and didn't finish the jug. He looked at his half-empty glass and remembered that other one he had left outside his house four days ago now. As he stood up, he momentarily lost his balance and had to cling to the back of his chair. He wished everyone a good night, and walked around the long table and up the stairs to bed.

It had been warm in the public room, but the temperature upstairs had plummeted, and even though Thomas spread three of the dampish wool blankets over him, it was a long time before he stopped feeling cold. The voices from downstairs seemed louder now. Then there was another bout of plate rattling, footsteps, and somewhat later, from another corner of the building, a radio and running water, and somewhere else again, the banging of a door and distant shouts.

Thomas woke early the next day, but he couldn't force himself to get up and drifted off again. When he awoke the second time, it was after nine. Over the past few nights, he'd had all sorts of dreams, some of them almost waking dreams, and during the day too he had been pursued by images, fantasies that seemed more real than the landscapes he was passing through. But this last night he had dreamed nothing at all, and while he washed himself at the small basin in the passageway, he felt that outside of this one moment, the dusty smell, the running water, the distant sounds from the cowshed and the kitchen, the gloomy light, and the cold of the metal tap as he turned it off, nothing else existed.

In the public room the shy little girl was about to sweep the floor. His breakfast was already on the table, and when Thomas sat down, the girl silently brought him a thermos of coffee and a small jug of warm milk. When he asked to settle up, she called her mother, who was busier than she had been the day before and didn't say much either. Thomas didn't dare leave a tip. He said thank you and went up to pack. It was after ten when he hit the trail.

The narrow path zigzagged up the slope. Here and there were a few fir trees dotted about, but the higher Thomas climbed, the barer the vegetation grew. Lines of rock showed through the slope. The gray-brown pastureland was full of humps and hollows, in some of the dips cotton grass grew out of the boggy ground, in others tarns had formed in whose water clumping strands of narrow leaves, some two or three feet long, seemed to hang like the hair of drowned women. The sky had clouded over, in the scattered light the karst looked almost white, the water in the tarns bottomless and black.

It was very quiet, only when Thomas was quite a long way up, he could hear dogs barking and cowbells far below, and when he turned to look, he saw a great herd of goats and cows being driven in the direction of the pass. Bringing up the rear were two horses with packsaddles piled high. Thomas sat down on a rock until the column had passed around a promontory, and silence returned.

As he climbed and climbed, he had a sense of going backward in time. Flowers that had withered at the altitude of the pass were in full bloom up here, some hadn't even opened yet. The flatter the terrain, the more difficult the going became. The cracked and furrowed limestone karst resembled a petrified sea. All over the broken rock were cracks, some of them measuring several yards in width and depth. In other places there were gentle slopes that suddenly fell away or culminated in narrow ridges and crests that Thomas had to cross on all fours. The sharp rocks scratched his hands and cut into his knees.

Progress was exhausting, and Thomas was forced to stop repeatedly to catch his breath, but he wanted to get on and waited until it was afternoon before taking a break to eat. The sky was now thickly clouded, and the light so uncertain that it no longer cast a shadow. When he got up to move on, he no longer knew which way he had come. He tried to orient himself by the panorama, but the peaks all looked the same, stacked one behind the other in every direction. He chose one and decided to keep heading toward it until he encountered a path. He was now totally concentrated on the terrain, every step, every handhold, as though he were in slow motion. He was trapped in a labyrinth of rock, but the vague fear he felt was not so much to do with that as with the thought that even if he should find a path, he would still be lost.

The cloud layer had come down and obscured the peaks. A cold wind chased scraps of mist across the plateau. The rocks seemed to be a little less fissured here, and Thomas stepped out, he needed to find a path before the fog closed in and made orientation impossible. He quivered even before he was aware of the crash, a wild fluttering and at the same moment something gray beside his foot, a panic movement. He pulled his foot back, lost his balance, and out of the corner of his eye he saw a gray bird fly away, before, overbalancing, he spun around and a crevasse opened before him. He rowed with his arms fumbling for support. For a moment he had the sensation of flying.

That morning, for the first time, Astrid became aware that Thomas was with her all along. Whatever she was doing, she had felt his eye on her, with every decision his agreement or disapproval. In the course of the last few days she had often felt as though she were acting for him, he the director telling her what to do, with one of those looks he had occasionally sent her way and that over the years she had learned to read. He had tolerated her behavior with the policeman with a smile; he had never been one for jealousy and had taken Astrid's occasional flirting with other men with an amused tolerance or a plain indifference that had offended her. He had always been certain of her, more than she of him, even though she would have been unable to come up with any grounds for doubting him. Maybe, she thought, her love was less strong than his, maybe her doubts regarding him were actually doubts of her own love.

Sometimes she felt he was far away, then he was standing behind her, and so close that she had the sensation of feeling the warmth of his body. She withstood the temptation to turn around and look for him. What shall I do? she asked him. Do you want me to look for you? Shall I follow you? Is it that you're waiting for me somewhere? Or shall I pretend nothing has happened? Do you need time? How much time? He didn't answer. Now even Manuela would have been welcome to Astrid with her clichés and her cheap comfort, but she had left last night, after telling herself a dozen times that her sister-in-law was doing better now, and that she would get through and no longer needed her help.

Astrid got up and went out onto the landing. There was the plastic bag with Thomas's clothes and shoes that the police had found in the shopping mall and delivered during the course of the day, while Astrid had been in the mountains looking for him. She felt the officials were making fun of her. Look, this is what's left of your husband, a crumpled shirt and a filthy pair of pants. Thus far, Thomas's disappearance had been in some way abstract, his absence not really different than when he'd been away at work or at his handball practice sessions. These discarded things were the first physical proof that he had taken himself out of their life together, that he would not return, and, naked as a newborn, had embarked on a new life alone. Astrid stuffed the old shoes and clothes into the trash, where Thomas had left them. But that wasn't enough. Though it was only half full, she took the bag out of the trash can, knotted it up, and carried it across to the school building, where the waste container stood. The idea that it would be picked up next week and put in the furnace along with the other stuff had something liberating about it.

The children were still asleep when she got back. Normally, she let them lie in on weekends, but she still felt the sense of being abandoned that she'd had when she woke up, so she went up to be with them. She slipped into bed with Ella and spooned with her. Her daughter's hair tickled her nose. Did you have a good sleep? she whispered. Ella yawned and stretched, and turned out of Astrid's embrace onto her back. Even though the girl tended to take after Thomas more, Astrid recognized herself in the movement. She lay there in the narrow bed and stretched luxuriously. The sky outside was cloudy, no one was about to send her out into the fresh air. Two days of lounging around in bed or on the sofa, reading and watching TV. Then she remembered her father, and her mother. She tried to think of something else, a book she'd read, plans she'd made with a girlfriend. Buying an old farmhouse with stables, keeping horses and chickens and rabbits, and having a lot of cats and a dog. Then they would live together, just the two of them, and do something amazing—she didn't have any precise idea of what it would be, but the whole world would love and admire her for it. Then from downstairs she heard her mother's voice, Get up, come along, you'll be late for school. But it was Saturday. And she hadn't had to go to school for years and years now. Ella turned away from Astrid, and pressed against her. What shall we do? asked Astrid. What about getting a dog? replied Ella.

Astrid had been afraid the children would be less able to cope with Thomas's absence than she, but it turned out to be the opposite. On that Saturday morning she had told them their father was doing fine, but that he would be gone for an unspecified time. It wasn't that he was unhappy with them, or with the family, it was a simple necessity. If their father had been a ship's captain, it would be completely normal for him to be gone for two or three months at a time. That idea seemed to make sense to the children: Their father was on a big trip, having adventures and seeing different parts of the world. And all the time he was thinking about them every day, and if he had been able to, then he would have sent them postcards too, or texts, or called them. But where he was, there were no postcards, no stamps, no mailboxes. And he had gone without his cell phone. Sometimes Konrad drew pictures of his father on a pirate ship, or a desert island, or at the top of a high mountain. When Astrid mentioned Thomas to them, both children reacted surprisingly apathetically, as though their chief interest was not to be robbed of their fantasies, even though they secretly knew that that's what they were.

The secretary from Thomas's place of work called several times and asked how he was doing, and if there wasn't a doctor's note. Finally Astrid was forced to make an appointment with his boss. When she walked in on the morning in question, the secretary greeted her with a hesitant smile and asked if Thomas was doing better. Astrid shook her head, and the secretary started talking about her mother's shingles again.

Thomas's boss hadn't been there for long. His predecessor had gone into retirement just a year ago, and there had been considerable competition for his job. In fact, the only one not to throw his hat into the ring had been Thomas, who said he'd rather work with his clients than deal with various personnel issues. In the end, the old boss had brought in an outsider to succeed him. The situation had resolved itself, but the new boss was not popular. Astrid felt relieved that she didn't have to talk to one of Thomas's long-term associates, most of whom she knew and with whose wives she went on company trips and other jollies.

The boss jumped up and stepped out to greet Astrid. Shall we sit at the low table? Would you like some coffee? Astrid declined and dropped into one of the low chairs around the table. Thomas has disappeared, she said quickly, to get it behind her. The boss looked at her inquiringly. What do you mean disappeared? Astrid explained the situation to him. She was surprised at how cool she sounded. The boss remained perfectly practical and offered no reaction. He suggested not telling any of the others for the moment. We'll just say he's sick. He won't be gone forever, after all. He's not coming back, said Astrid. The boss looked at her, as though he thought that was her wish. I'm sure he's not coming back, she said. Well, let's just wait and see for now, said the boss. We'll continue to pay his salary during the normal severance period. And so long as it's not more than a month or two, we can treat the whole thing as time out, a sabbatical. In view of Thomas's long service, there's nothing out of the ordinary about that.

Astrid hadn't even thought about the money. While she slunk through reception, hoping not to run into the secretary again, she calculated that by November at the latest the company would stop paying his salary. Thomas had always dealt with their money matters, after all that was his job. He didn't earn badly, but they hadn't any great savings salted away, and there was a mortgage on the house.

Astrid spent the rest of the morning trying to gain an insight into their financial position and to estimate how long they would manage to survive on their reserves. The sums left her confused and frightened, until eventually she scooped up all the papers and stuffed them back into Thomas's desk drawer.

What she would most have liked would be if no one else had known about Thomas's disappearance. But of course Manuela had to mention it to her parents. Thomas's mother had phoned. She didn't even seem to be that alarmed. In the course of a long and mostly nonsensical conversation, she tried to apologize for her son's behavior. She related episodes from his childhood that Astrid had heard dozens of times, talked about Thomas's problems with authority, his thick skull, his obstinacy, as though Astrid didn't know all that herself, and as though it could explain anything. At the end of their conversation, Thomas's mother claimed that he would be back soon, and it was all just a misunderstanding, probably. Astrid didn't even bother to argue with her. If we can do anything to help, she said. Thank you, said Astrid, I'll call you if I need anything. After that she heard nothing more from Thomas's parents. Manuela called from time to time offering her help and sending her best wishes from the parents. We're fine, said Astrid, thanks all the same, but we're doing fine. She hadn't told her own parents anything, and one time when visiting them, she dinned it into the children not to say anything either. Astrid's mother asked how Ella and Konrad would like to spend a few days in the fall vacation with them. The children were thrilled, but Astrid rudely turned down the offer. Are you going away then? asked her mother. I don't know yet, said Astrid, we don't know.

Patrick hadn't called since the aborted search. So Astrid was surprised to see him standing outside the door one afternoon in late September with a solemn expression on his face. Even before she could ask him inside, he said, We've found him.

Thomas's initial sensation was of a burning pain. Thereafter cold and damp. He was lying bent double on a sloping surface, his whole body hurt. He tried not to move, producing in his mind an index of everything that hurt him, from superficial things that felt like scrapes and cuts, to his throbbing ankle and shoulder, and a deafening pain in his head, dull sensations in his hands and feet, which felt like shapeless lumps. Then there were little pinpricks of snowflakes falling on his face, tiny contacts. When he opened his eyes, he saw that he was lying on a wide and fairly deep shelf of rock. He must have fallen twelve or fifteen feet. The slice of sky over him was gray with falling snow and the oncoming dark. It was eerily quiet. Thomas thought about the snow grouse that had caused his fall. He asked himself how it managed to survive in such bleak country, where it found anything to eat in winter when everything was covered with snow, how and where it spent its time. Cautiously he twisted his head first one way then the other, and as he did so, he realized he was lying on the little mossy, ferny spot he had glimpsed while falling. Next to him was a little outcrop of rock, and the crack narrowed and led on down. Everything was thinly covered with snow, his jacket was ripped, and there were dark bloodstains on his pants. Cautiously he pulled himself up, moved first his arms, then his legs. He seemed not to have any major injuries.

His ankle was swollen, but presumably sprained, not broken. He had abrasions over a wide area but no deep wounds. His head hurt, possibly he had a concussion. He kept thinking he might easily have died, but he pushed the thought away in order to be able to concentrate on the moment and on the danger in which he still found himself. When he stood up, he felt so dizzy that he had to grab hold of the cold rock. He swung his arms back and forth like pendulum weights until the feeling returned to his hands. His first impulse was to climb out of the crack right away, but after brief reflection, he decided to spend the night down here, where he would at least be slightly protected from the weather. He wouldn't have been able to go for long in the dark over the karst with his damaged ankle. If he pressed himself right up against the cliff, he was hidden under a small overhang. He spread his rain jacket over him, and ate bread and dried fruit and a whole bar of chocolate. He didn't drink much, though, he needed to economize on his water, he only had half a flask. After eating, he rolled himself up and tried to sleep. The heavy snowflakes landed on the thin material of his jacket with faint sounds like little sighs.

He spent the greater part of the night in a state between sleeping and waking. His mind was churning, images surfaced that were more like dreams, and then for moments at a time he knew only pain and cold and exhaustion. His jacket grew heavy with snow. Thomas tried to think of home, his warm bed, Astrid and the kids. But the scenes escaped him, he saw mountains lit from within under a starless sky, he flew up never-ending sheer surfaces, so close to the rock that he could make out the tiniest details. He was sustained by an air current that picked him up and dropped him, but even when he fell he didn't lose control, he fell and fell down along the vertical wall. Then he was suddenly wide awake and could feel only cold and pain and the hard rock beneath. He had to get up and move around. He pushed back the jacket and saw that it had stopped snowing. It was completely dark in his little crevasse, but there were stars in the sky. He took the headlamp out of his rucksack and saw that his watch had stopped at half past seven. It must have been damaged in the fall, the casing was scratched and the glass cracked. Although there were no indications that the night was nearly over, he began to clamber up the wall. His headlamp lit only a small circle that trembled up and down in front of him. He climbed slowly and cautiously, testing every hold before trusting it. The rock was wet and slippery, snow had settled on little ledges and in cracks that now burned his fingertips. It took a long time before he reached the top and hauled himself up over the rim. He knelt in the snow and directed the beam of his light like a searchlight in the nearest vicinity. Then he switched it off, to force his eyes to adjust to the darkness.

The starry sky was of an overpowering beauty, the stars seeming to vibrate with cold. Even though there was a half-moon the barren waste of the landscape was surprisingly easy to see, it was as though the snow was giving off a pallid illumination. Even so, Thomas set himself to wait for it to get light before moving off.

The terrain was still gently uphill. Thomas wanted to reach the highest point, where he would surely find a marker. No more than six or eight inches of snow had come down overnight, but it was enough to make progress appreciably harder than the day before. The snow blanketed the uneven terrain, and small hollows and cracks were barely discernible.

The sun had yet to crest the horizon, but the sky was already light. The snow had lost its luminosity, it just looked gray now, and much darker than in the night. His sprained ankle hurt, and Thomas walked very slowly, stopping frequently. Finally, on the horizon before him, he saw a cairn of stones. He felt so relieved that for a moment all strength drained out of him, and he almost sank to his knees. On the wide plateau there were several six-foot piles of rock like sentries staring out in all directions. From the tallest of them a rusty iron cross poked out, and next to it were yellow markers, one of which pointed him back down to the pass, another to an upland farm an hour away. Between two stones in the cairn was a discolored tin can that contained a summit book—a simple ring binder and a ballpoint pen. Thomas turned the pages of the binder. Some climbers had just entered their name and the date, others made a note of the route they had walked, while others again had offered a comment: the beauty of God's earth, we'll be back, fog all day, reached the top much too late. The newest entry was a week old, just a single name in spidery handwriting. Thomas tried to work out what day of the week it was, but he couldn't be sure, and finally just put his name.

As he was descending to the farm, the sun rose and it got so bright that he had to shut his eyes against the glare. Farther down, where the limestone scree gradually gave way to pastureland and the terrain flattened out, the snow was only half as deep as on the exposed summit, and in some places he saw bunches of grass poking through it.

It took him twice as long to the alp as the marker had promised. Finally, though, he saw a long cow barn and a small hut beside it, which he soon reached. The lower floor was of quarry stone, the wood above was old and weathered, only the fiber-cement roof seemed to have been replaced recently. The windows were shuttered, but the door wasn't bolted. Hesitantly, Thomas stepped in. It was colder inside than out. It took a while for his eyes to get used to the dark. Even after he had pushed open all the shutters, it didn't make much difference.

The hut seemed to have been abandoned for the winter. He looked around. The room was sparsely furnished, apart from a table with a corner bench and a few chairs, there was a two-ring gas cooker and a kitchen unit above it. Thomas hoped he might find something to eat, but the cupboard contained only a few spice jars, a box of sugar cubes, some packets of various teas and a half-full jar of Nescafé. Next to the table was a wood-burning stove, in a corner a large wooden chest containing blankets, some items of clothing, and various odds and ends in sealed plastic boxes. Above it was a wall shelf with maps, walking guides, books on the flora and fauna of the region, and a few novels. There were also board games, a set of playing cards, and a leather tumbler with a pair of dice. On the walls there was a walking map of the area, a few children's drawings, and photographs, all showing the same woman, now sitting in the sun outside the hut, now scaling a rock, now milking a goat, now herding a few cows. In the back wall of the hut was a locked door. Thomas went through the chest and the kitchen cupboard and finally found the key in an old cracked cup full of thumbtacks and rubber bands.

The back room was even darker. From there a steep flight of steps led upstairs where there was a tiny bedroom on the mountain side, and at the front a slightly bigger one. The mattresses had been stood up against the wall, the woolen blankets hanging on lines. Climbing back down he noticed a second door, behind which was a chemical toilet and a big wooden box resembling a sea chest. He lifted the lid and saw by the light of his lighter all kinds of dry goods, rice, noodles, sugar, salt, cans with vegetables, and even meat. There were some bottles of wine, and three one-liter bottles containing a clear liquid; according to the handwritten labels these contained *träsch*, the local fruit brandy.

Thomas went out into the open to look around. Slightly above the hut was a small lake; the water was perfectly clear, but he couldn't see the bottom. The cow barn, which was slightly below the hut, was narrow but fully thirty yards in length. In the hayloft, Thomas found fence posts and staples with rolls of yellow twine and a big pile of kindling. He carried an armload of wood back into the hut and lit a fire in the stove. But it wouldn't draw, no sooner had Thomas lit it than the room filled with acrid smoke. He threw open the door and windows. Outside he saw that up on the roof, a plank had been laid across the chimney opening.

By noon there was a fire going in the stove, and the hut was toasty warm. Thomas was eating noodles with a ready-made tomato sauce he had found in the food chest. After lunch he sat on the bench outside the hut in the sun. Again, he was amazed by the absolute silence. From the east, clouds were getting up.

In the afternoon Thomas lugged as much wood as he could carry into the hut. He was still at work when it began to snow, and it was still snowing when he stepped outside late at night, to smoke one of his last cigarettes. He had spent the evening drawing up a list of all the food he had. He had drunk some of the powerful *träsch*, which had gone to his head in no time at all. As he climbed the steps to bed, he had to grab hold of the balustrade so as not to fall.

The ice-cold bedroom was so tiny that Thomas had the sense he was lying in a box. Though tired and a little drunk, he couldn't get to sleep for a long time. He lay in bed, staring into the darkness. When he shut his eyes, everything seemed to spin, and he saw this image in his mind's eye: himself lying at the bottom of the crevasse, spread-eagled and with shattered limbs. It was as though he was a long way up, staring down at the torpid body lying there, covered with snow and with an unnatural smile etched into the rigid face, the smile of a dead man.

Among all the thoughts that filled Astrid's mind in the next few days, there was one that never let go of her: that this was not necessarily real, rather just one among many possibilities. Sometimes she thought it was something she had in her power, to decide in favor of one or other of these possibilities. Thomas's death was the simplest because it was so specific, so unambivalent and clear. A hiker loses his footing, takes a fall, and is dead on the spot. How many times she had seen such reports in the papers without really taking them in. And then every year the statistics of deaths in the Alps, neatly compiled, a hundred and fifty, two hundred incidents, distributed among the various types of accident, rockfall, icefall, avalanche, slip.

Thomas had fallen, no one could say quite how or why. Presumably he had died as a result of his fall. Perhaps not right away, perhaps he had bled to death, or frozen or died of thirst, the autopsy would provide clarity on that. It had snowed overnight, an early onset of winter of the sort that was not unusual at that altitude. Snow had sheeted over the corpse, but after a few icy days there was a break in the weather, the snow melted, and huntsmen had found the body. If a shred of his jacket hadn't got caught at the rim of the crevasse, he might never have been found, or not for fifty or a hundred years, when Astrid and even the children would be long gone.

All the details were in the police report, the place, date, and time of the find, even the names and addresses of those who had made it. There was confirmation that Thomas had spent the night before the accident in the dormitory on the pass and had entered his name in the summit log. It must have been during the descent, perhaps he had gained his objective and had turned around and was on his way home. Later, there would be more detailed medical reports, the manner and gravity of his injuries, the presumed cause of death. There was a body that had been found by people with names, professions, and families; there were clothes and shoes and a rucksack with food and a few pieces of hiking gear. All these were facts being brought to bear, but what did they signify? Anything, the merest trifle, and everything could have happened differently. If, on that last day of the vacation, Thomas and not Astrid had gone up to see to Konrad, if she had checked the banking transactions earlier, if the police dog had had more stamina. The tiniest detail, the least circumstance was enough to split reality in two, in four, eight, sixteen versions, into an unending number of worlds.

Thomas had disappeared a month ago. From the very beginning, Astrid had sensed he wasn't coming back. His death was the simplest solution; it cleared away all possible questions, removed all the issues, the reason for Thomas's disappearance, the road he had chosen, why he had used his credit card even though he must have known it would lead to his discovery, why he had written his name in the summit log. Nor would anyone now want to hear Astrid's own confused and contradictory explanations, her lies and evasions. Thomas's work colleagues would offer their sympathy to the bereaved family, stand around uselessly at the funeral, and at the wake sit at a separate table, swapping stories about him. His parents and Manuela would tell stories, his friends from the handball team, the neighbors, simple stories that were supposed to keep him alive, keep his memory green, but in fact over the years would come to stand in for him and finally, ironically, cause him to disappear.

Astrid thought of a different version. Thomas hadn't died of his fall, he had merely ripped his jacket and sustained a slight injury. He had clambered up out of the crevasse and walked back to the pass. When the huntsmen found the shred of material weeks later, it was nothing of significance. By then Thomas had completely disappeared. She looked for a map to see where he might have gone. There was the pass, on the road map with its scale of one to three hundred thousand, but the area of scree to the southeast was just an expanse of white with some gray shadings to suggest its topography. The names of the peaks, the various altitudes, the names of places and the colored roads, highways, and motorways were just claims, more facts that wouldn't be translated into any reality and would only make Astrid sad. She folded up the map and closed her eyes. Now she could see Thomas climbing out of the crevasse and walking over the plateau; he was walking with a limp, but he was walking fast. He stopped to eat something at an Alpine hut, and walked on over snowy pastures. The track gave way to an unmade road and then a narrow paved mountain road. Thomas was walking through a fir wood down into a valley. The snow had given way to rain, he was freezing, but he was energized by his scrape with death. It was just beginning to get dark when he came to a village, a bleak-looking place in a narrow valley. He found an inn, and ate and drank. The heat wasn't on in his room, no one was expecting a visitor so late in the day. Even though the landlady had said the rooms were all nonsmoking, there was a smell of cold smoke and air freshener. Thomas switched on the TV and slid under the thick down comforter. The late news came on, reports of conflicts, crises, catastrophes, but nothing could disturb Thomas's contentment. He was safe and everything to him was delicious, every color, every sound, every word. He was alive.

Thomas awoke with a headache. It was dark in the room, but a few slivers of dazzling light pierced the cracks in the shutters. When he got up, he felt faint and was forced to sit down again. After the dizzy feeling had left him, he got up again and walked slowly and carefully down the stairs. Every step he took seemed to hurt his head. He lit the stove and put water for coffee on the gas burner. He put away the half-empty bottle of *träsch*; the very sight of it seemed to bring on his headache.

After drinking two cups of coffee with a lot of sugar, he felt better and stepped outside. The sun was shining, but a foot of snow had fallen overnight. Thomas's footprints from the day before were covered, the landscape shone white and intact, as though it was a new world that had come into being overnight. He started to wonder what it would be like to spend the winter here, with the lake frozen over and snow to a depth of many feet. He would only be able to leave the hut via an upstairs window and couldn't move without the help of skis or snowshoes. His supplies of food would only keep him for two or three months, and the wood and gas would probably run out long before that. He studied the map on the wall. Even going back to the pass now would be treacherous, with snow blanketing the cloven limestone karst and concealing the holes, and yet not firm enough to take his weight. All he could see around him were mountains and uninhabited valleys, the nearest village was a day's walk away. He had every reason to feel anxious, but he was happy. The hut didn't feel like a prison to him; on the contrary, he felt free here in a way he had rarely felt before. And he had the absurd feeling he could survive the winter even without food, so long as he moved quietly and unobtrusively like the animals who stuck it out here, somehow, and lived on god knows what.

The days passed imperceptibly in aimless busywork. Thomas was never short of things to do. He carried wood to the hut, fetched water from the little lake, made sure the fire never went out. He cooked on the gas burner, and after the gas ran out, on the wood-burning stove. He cleaned the hut, got more wood from the cow barn, mixed up dough, and after several failed attempts, managed to bake a sort of flatbread. It was cold, but when the sun shone, its warmth was so intense that he could sit in front of the hut in his shirtsleeves, whittling crude figures from firewood or reading one of the books he had found. The fantasy worlds of novels did nothing for him, but he studied the books about plant and animal life, and learned that marmots and chamois lived around here, and snow hares, eagles, black grouse, and Alpine snow grouse. The male of the snow grouse, so he was informed, molted four times a year, the female three times. They put such faith in their perfected camouflage that they didn't take flight until the very last moment, when you were about to step on them, and then they would pretend to be injured, to lure the invader away from the nest. They mimed their injury so well, wrote the author, that even he would fall for it every time. In a book about the valley, Thomas read that hunters must have come into the area shortly after the last ice age. In some of the innumerable caves thousand-year-old animal bones were found, bearing traces of human workmanship. Some of the Alps had been planed away for hundreds of years. The book had stories of folk customs, freak weather events and natural catastrophes, and life in the Alps. Sometimes it might happen, he read somewhere, that herdsmen would forget a goat in the Silberen or be unable to find it. If the animal managed to survive the winter, then, come spring, it would have lost its entire covering of hair through lack of salt.

Thomas hadn't been keeping track of the days, but he must have been on the mountain for a week when the foehn winds set in, and the temperature leapt up overnight. In the space of a single day the snow almost completely melted away. Everywhere now were the sounds of thaw, a dripping and gurgling from the roof, a plashing and rushing and pouring. In among it were the distant occasional clangs of cowbells from a pasture much lower on the mountain. Once, when he smoked his very last cigarette outside the hut before going to bed, he heard a long-held yelping and shortly afterward the murmured benediction of the Alpsegen.

Every day Thomas had rubbed his sprained ankle with schnapps. The swelling had gone down, the pain had eased, and he felt sufficiently strong to begin to reconnoiter. His circles grew wider by the day. The hut lay at the edge of a flat hollow from whose edge one could see far down into a barren valley. Thomas climbed a narrow side valley, bounded on one side by a tall, apparently unscalable cliff. At its foot was a gigantic scree, and in the valley bottom, perhaps half an hour away, was a substantial lake with turquoise water that was so clear when you approached that you could count the stones on the bottom. By the lake's edge were scraps of snow, but the water was less cold than Thomas had anticipated. He swam a few strokes and then sat on a rock to dry out. A gentle breeze cooled his skin, burning in the sun. While he ate his pack lunch, he looked around. On the horizon, between the limestone peak in the north and the cliff to the south, there was a crossing, a broad saddle of moraine. After Thomas had rested, he walked on in the direction of the saddle. The path was longer and steeper than he had thought, it was hard to judge distance in the treeless, featureless terrain. Even before he had reached it, he heard a gunshot ricocheting off the rocks and seeming to rumble at him from every side. He scanned the area, but saw no human being, no animal, nothing moving. Even so, he turned around and set off for home. He was almost there when he heard two more shots, one after the other. The last stretch he was almost running. He was afraid the hunter might track him down to his hiding place like a wild animal.

It was as though the hunters' appearance had broken a spell, Thomas's feeling of security was gone, and he understood how exposed he was up here. Even if the hunters didn't find him, it could get cold again at any moment and start snowing, and the next lot of snow would probably stay there and not melt until springtime. That afternoon he took down the chimney and covered the opening in the roof with the piece of board. He closed the shutters and didn't leave the hut without first peeking through the cracks to check that the coast was clear. In the evening, he packed his rucksack.

Astrid afterward could hardly remember the initial period of grieving. The episodes of it were so visceral and so detached from everything else that she was unable to incorporate them into a chronology of her life. Sadness was like a body of water, indivisible, and she kept falling into it. She was incapable of thinking, incapable of feeling, incapable of breath; she dissolved in the heaviness of this other element; nor did time itself have any significance, it seemed not to exist. Nothing could get through to her; her spirit was encapsulated in her body, which continued to function by itself. She looked after the children mechanically, almost without noticing them. Each time that she resurfaced and it was all over, as unexpectedly as it had begun, all that remained in her was a dull sense of exhaustion.

Everyone offered help and support, above all, everyone wanted to talk about it with her: her parents, Thomas's parents, Manuela, friends, and neighbors. Astrid didn't want to talk. She did what she had to do, what she was called upon to do. She talked to the minister, organized a funeral, sent out death announcements, replied to letters of condolence. She talked to the authorities, the bank, filled in forms, made calls, put Thomas's affairs in order. She held on to these concrete tasks, the illusion that even a fatality could be settled, that processes existed that could restore order to chaos. And all the time she had the feeling of watching herself from outside, as though she were playing a part in someone's movie that had nothing to do with her life.

The children's grief was more insidious than Astrid's, but thereby all the more profound, like an illness that over the years almost imperceptibly weakens and finally destroys the human body. The teachers had addressed their classes and asked them to show utmost consideration. Konrad's classmates had given him a large sheet of paper on which each one of them had drawn a flower and sent him a good wish. Ella had come home with a number of brightly colored notes and had shown some of them to Astrid, awkward sympathy notes, written in glitter pen and plastered with weeping hearts and little stuck-down animal shapes. Ella had looked mutely at her mother, as though to ask what she should do. And they gave me some chocolate as well, said Ella. That's okay, said Astrid, and put the cards back in their gaudy envelopes. They didn't mean any harm by it.

With Christmas coming up, and Astrid in reasonable shape, all seemed well. The children drew up lists of Christmas wishes and made presents for their grandparents and godparents. Ella was rehearsing a part in the school nativity play, and Konrad helped Astrid bake cookies. Their disturbance showed itself in different ways, after the holidays were over, during the rain and chill of January and February. Ella read more than ever, and was quieter and quieter. She threw herself into her schoolwork as though her life depended on getting good grades and getting a place in the gymnasium.

Meanwhile, Konrad, who had always been a good pupil, seemed to give up and became troublesome, often acting cheeky to his mother and sister, and his teacher.

Sometimes for hours or days on end, they were all one heart and one soul, for instance when they watched a film on TV on Friday evening, or visited the grandparents, when they went on a trip to the Ticino over Easter, to friends who had invited them repeatedly and had been put off time and time again. Then they were able to behave as though this was how it was supposed to be, and they enjoyed themselves. Astrid didn't notice how many sweets the children ate, how long they played computer games, or what time they went to bed. So long as they were content.

On the advice of the school psychologist, she sent Konrad to a therapist. But it did little to change his behavior, and after a couple of sessions, he refused to go anymore. Only after he'd gone up a grade in the new school year and had a young woman teacher who had only just qualified did he calm down, and his performance started to improve. Joining a judo club and attending twice-weekly practice sessions seemed to help as well. But there was always a shadow hanging over Ella and Konrad, an indefinable air of sadness and reserve. Sometimes Astrid would come upon the children sitting vacantly in their rooms, lost in thoughts they either wouldn't or couldn't share with her.

Sometime that summer, as though Astrid's family and friends had consulted with one another while her back was turned, she felt a growing impatience from her surroundings, some expectation that she settle down, think of herself, and begin to look for a new partner. As if it was her duty to forget Thomas and make a fresh start. Almost a year had passed since his death, she was only forty-four, a good-looking woman, and it would be better for the children too to have a father. They have one, said Astrid. No one seemed to understand that her relationship with Thomas wasn't over just because he wasn't around anymore.

Without having intended to, she was living a double life. She got through her day, packed the children off to school, kept the house tidy, cooked, gardened, helped Ella with her homework, which was harder now that she was in secondary school, and took Konrad to judo. She played with the children, chatted with the neighbors, went swimming most mornings when the kids were at school, to plow up and down a few lanes. But in bed at night, when she couldn't sleep, she would think about Thomas and was perfectly sure he wasn't dead. It was less a thought than a feeling. A thought was something she might have been able to oppose with facts, but this she couldn't overturn. She didn't want to either; it helped her more than grief, which made nothing better, explained nothing, was no help and no proof. Her nightly fantasies were no wish-fulfillment images either, invented by her to comfort herself. Thomas was gone, there was no doubting that, but he wasn't dead. She saw him walking through deserted landscapes, seeking shelter under the jutting eaves of roofs, or in gas stations, or chapels. He was buying food in small general stores, sat in bars all by himself, spent the night in cheap pensions or haylofts. When he needed money, he did temporary work, helped a farmer with the harvest, worked on a chicken farm, did the dishes in a restaurant. After a few weeks he moved on, on foot, never mind the weather.

Once, he was picked up by the police. He had attracted their attention by walking along the highway in the rain. The patrol car had drawn up alongside him, and the officer in the front passenger seat, who resembled Patrick, asked him if everything was all right and asked to see his ID. But Thomas's name was no longer on the wanted files, for everyone bar Astrid his case was closed.

She didn't talk to anyone about her fantasies, not because she was afraid they would think she was crazy but because she wanted to keep these scenes to herself, not share them with anyone else. She thought that Thomas was probably alive for Ella and Konrad as well. She had no other explanation for the fact that the children never wanted to talk about their father, and would either go quiet or else run away if Astrid so much as mentioned him. They never wanted to accompany her to the cemetery to tend his grave. The more time passed, the less she believed he was actually there. She felt like a swindler, a cheat, going to tend an empty grave.

She had uprooted a few blown primroses and dropped them in the compost. As she planted fresh heather, she heard Thomas's voice as though he were standing directly behind her: Don't bother with that, he said, that's no good to either of us. Come along. She stood up and left the cemetery, went out onto the street. Only when she reached the station did it dawn on her that this was her childhood village, that the barrier had not yet been replaced by an underpass, that the storehouse that burned down one night was still standing, and so was the old villa next to the post office, with the tangled garden. When Thomas told people about how they had first met, Astrid would always claim that she couldn't remember, but now she saw the scene distinctly in front of her. It was spring, she had started on her apprenticeship just a few weeks before, and she wasn't used to the long working days yet. She was in the back room, unpacking the new orders, when the bell rang. Her boss had stepped out to get something, so Astrid went out to serve whoever it was. In the middle of the store—as though he wanted not to get too close to the books—stood a young man, barely older than she was. He went up to the desk and said he was looking for the civil law book and the part about the Code of Obligations. We'd have to order that for you, said Astrid. The boss had briefly walked her through the catalogue of books in print, but she didn't really know her way around it, and it took her a while before she found it, and filled in an order form. She could feel Thomas looking at her, and every time she looked up he was smiling at her and nodding encouragingly. She asked him for his name and address. And then he asked her for hers. Astrid in Wonderland, he said. No, she said, you're thinking of Alice. Oh, right, he said, I never read it. Me neither, said Astrid, and laughed. But you'd rather read law books anyway, she said, serious things. I won't read that either, he said, I just need it for the trainee school. What books do you read? *The House of the Spirits* by Isabel Allende, said Astrid. What's that about? Everything under the sun, she said and laughed again. It's a family history over three generations. It's not a book men would like. So what would she recommend for him? asked Thomas. She stepped out from behind the desk, and while she led him up to one of the shelves, she played the bookseller. She felt foolish, dancing about in front of him, pulling books off the shelves and telling him the plots, but she couldn't help herself. In the end, Thomas bought a book, one of the Maigrets that she recommended, after he had told her he liked books with a bit of excitement to them. She couldn't shake the feeling that he was just buying it for her sake. Once you've read it, will you come and tell me how you liked it?

Thomas spent the winter in the Gotthard area. For the first few days he was put up by a Capuchin monk who was in charge of two small parishes down in the valley. He was a kindly man and very busy. He asked no questions and helped Thomas find work with a carpenter in the village. Thomas wasn't especially good with his hands, but the carpenter had a large order to fill from a nearby ski resort and was glad of the cheap labor. Thomas found lodgings with an old widow, who let a couple of rooms to long-term tenants. The house was at the bottom of a narrow valley and got practically no sun in the winter. The poorly lit rooms never got properly warm and had a sour dusty smell. The other tenants were a retiree and a young teaching assistant who was just doing her final bit of in-post training. By the time Thomas got off work, it would be dark already, and when he walked into the sitting room and turned on the light, the retiree would often be there. The first time, Thomas thought he must have woken him, but then he noticed that the old fellow liked to sit in the dark fully awake, as though hiding or lying in wait for something or someone. Thomas showered, then he would take a stroll through the village or go up to his room until it was dinnertime. The widow was very parsimonious, forever reminding Thomas to turn off the lights when he left a room, or to switch off the heat at night. In the room beside his was the young teacher, who had introduced herself to him simply as Priska. Over dinner she talked animatedly about her pupils and colleagues. Sometimes the widow would put in, What was the name of that teacher who would let the kids go five minutes early, or, Is the headmaster's wife still in charge of the library? Then she would inform them that one woman was the daughter of the stationmaster who lived in the yellow house at the end of the village, that his wife was the baker's sister and had MS, that the teacher's brother had studied in the seminary in Lucerne but had gotten married and was now working in an advertising agency in Zurich, endless tangled family histories that Thomas instantly got lost in and was left with the impression that everyone here was related by blood or marriage or both. Sometimes the widow would talk about her gifted son, who worked in finance and was living in London. She spoke in raptures about him and his achievements and his huge salary, but Thomas couldn't help feeling she would have liked it better if he had stayed in the village and led a modest life close by.

On weekends Priska took off into the lowlands, and even though Thomas only ever saw her at mealtimes during the week, he would miss her. When he heard her returning late on Sunday night, going up to her room and then the bathroom that the three of them shared, he had a sensation of safety and warmth.

In the mornings, Thomas was always the first to use the bathroom. He hadn't shaved since his departure, and by now his beard was so long that his face looked strange to him in the mirror, and older than he thought it ought to be.

He had taken the half-full bottle of *träsch* with him out of the hut. It was in his closet, but he didn't touch it. He no longer drank alcohol, not from any resolution, he simply had no desire to intoxicate himself. He had given up reading too, even the paper. He didn't switch on the portable radio that was in his room, even music struck him as basically a distraction. Work at the carpenter's he enjoyed, repetitive though it was. He liked the monotony of the days, the set procedures, the morning rides out to the building site in Urserental, lunch with his colleagues, always at the same table in the same restaurant, and the evening rides down the Schöllenen Gorge into the sunless valley.

At the end of November Priska had her birthday. She announced it quite casually over dinner: By the way, it's my birthday today. Everyone offered congratulations, and after dinner the widow fetched a carton of vanilla ice cream out of the freezer, full of ice crystals and tasting of cardboard. That seemed to be the end of it. But after they had all taken their plates into the kitchen and stacked them in the dishwasher, and the widow and the retiree had installed themselves in the living room in front of the TV, Priska asked if Thomas felt like going out for a beer with her. Her treat. They crept out of the house, as though they were doing something illegal.

Thomas was no longer used to making conversation. Apart from the carpenter and his colleagues, who gave him instructions and passed comments on his work, he didn't tend to speak much. At mealtimes too he preferred to listen. At first Priska seemed not to notice his silence, she had so much to say herself, but after ordering the second round of beers, there was a moment of silence. Then she asked, Are you always this quiet? I don't know, said Thomas. I don't have much to say for myself. You're from the east of the country, aren't you? Yes, from Thurgau. Have you got family? He hesitated, as though he had to think about it. Yes, he said then, with a little crack in his voice, as though he was surprised by his answer. He saw in Priska's eyes that she wanted to ask him more. What about you, he asked her, have you got a boyfriend? Sort of, she said reluctantly. Guess how old I am? It was her thirtieth birthday, so they had to drink three beers each, one for each decade. Or shall we make it one for each year? asked Priska laughing. The alcohol was getting to Thomas. It wasn't even ten o'clock when he said he had to go, he had to get up early.

On the way home, Priska was telling him her hobby was kitesurfing, and since Thomas hadn't heard of that, she had to explain to him what it was. All the lights were out in the pension. They spoke in whispers and crept through the dark house to their rooms. Last year I went kitesurfing in Ireland, Priska whispered quickly. On Achill Island, off the west coast, do you want to see pictures?

They sat together on the bed, Priska had her laptop on her knees and showed him photographs of a bleak-looking landscape. A lake with surfers on it, hanging on to dirigible kites, being towed over the surface, most of them so far away you could barely make them out. Other than that, there were no people in the pictures, just scruffy-looking sheep with black faces and splotches of color on their fleece, whole herds of them or else single mothers with their lambs. Little white cottages dotted the outsize landscape, ruined barns, cobbled-together fences, high cliffs, and at the foot of them the sea, an endless plain that lost itself on the horizon against the brightness of the sky. The landscape attracted Thomas, it seemed to be a place of farewells and arrivals, both.

Although it wasn't warm in the room, Priska had taken off her sweater. Underneath she was wearing a sleeveless T-shirt. The lace trim of her bra showed through the thin cotton. Thomas could feel the pressure of her upper arm against his and her hand, holding the laptop, on his thigh. He could smell Priska's hair, her body, a hint of soap. He turned to face her. She didn't take her eyes off the screen, but in her poise there was tension, as though she was expecting a powerful movement. He kissed her throat and felt a shiver go through her.

Thomas lay in bed. It was past midnight, but he couldn't sleep. He thought about Astrid, about how they had met and then lost each other from sight. The time he first walked into the bookstore, he had fallen instantly in love with her, and from then on he had regularly gone to the shop to see her. He had never been a great reader, but the pleasure of their conversations was recompense for the labor of reading. To begin with, she recommended thrillers for him, but over time she trusted him with harder books as well, classics, or new novels and stories that he read conscientiously to be able to talk about them with her the following week. He had been pretty shy at the time, and never dared ask her to go out with him, or even to go for a coffee. Perhaps he was satisfied with their meetings in the usually empty bookstore, and they were in a sense more intimate than encounters in any public space could have been. When the owner saw Thomas walk in, she would call Astrid, who was usually working in the back room. It's your customer, she would call out with a smile, before disappearing into the back room to leave them alone. Sometimes Thomas had the impression the bookstore only existed for him and Astrid, a cryptic meeting place in a world that otherwise was far too bright and loud.

With their reading, their conversations changed. After they had both read Erich Fromm's *The Art of Loving*, they spent weeks discussing love and relationships. Thomas would have liked to think that mature love wasn't based on sex, and that it wasn't love for a single being but for the whole world, but everything in him was at odds with the views of the distinguished psychologist. You love what you take trouble over, and you take trouble over what you love, said Astrid, and to him that was like a secret message he wasn't sure he understood.

Things could have gone on like that for ages if Astrid hadn't one day told him about a boyfriend she was going to Italy with for the summer holiday. He had always thought it was too soon to declare his love; now it was too late. All through the summer he thought about what he would say to Astrid when he saw her next, but when he finally saw her again at the end of August, tanned and fresh and laughing, he didn't manage to say anything at all. Instead, he bought the book she recommended to him, *The Beautiful Summer* by Cesare Pavese, and scoured it in the following week for secret messages.

For a time they both moved in the same circle of friends. Thomas suffered when he saw Astrid with her boyfriend, but when he didn't see her, he suffered worse. Then he finished his traineeship and had to do his national military service. When he returned to the village, Astrid had moved to the city with her boyfriend. Thomas started working for the company where he had been a trainee. He was loosely in touch with Astrid; they wrote each other postcards on holiday and from time to time short letters full of ordinary day-to-day stuff and phrases. When Astrid was in the village visiting her parents, they would sometimes run into each other at parties or just on the street. By this time, Thomas was involved with someone himself, a halfhearted thing with a woman in the handball club he had joined. He tried without much success to justify his lack of love by Erich Fromm's philosophy. When the woman moved on after a year or so, he still suffered like a dog.

On her twenty-fifth birthday, Astrid had a party and invited Thomas. That evening he learned that she had broken up with her boyfriend and was single again. He took the plunge and asked her out for dinner.

There were good days and bad days. The grief didn't get any less, but it came over Astrid less often. Sometimes she wouldn't think about Thomas for whole days at a time, only at night in bed, when she imagined sleeping with him. It was always the same scene, she was lying on the bed, Thomas kneeling beside her. Neither of them spoke. He carefully undressed her, as though unpacking a sensitive instrument. He would keep stopping to look at her or touch her, as though to convince himself that she was real. They were both smiling. Then he took his clothes off and lay on top of her. Their movements were slow, it was as though they were talking to each other, not alternatingly in a dialog but in a language in which they spoke the sentences together, and the sentences were at once question and answer. When Astrid shut her eyes, she had the sensation of being utterly filled by Thomas. As her excitement gradually ebbed, his image dulled, dissolving in the darkness until all that was left of him was a kind of halo, and once that was gone too, a vast emptiness that seemed to draw everything out of her.

The very first time they slept together, Astrid had come, even though they had both been wound up. They had gone to the movies and then to a pub. They hadn't had much to drink because Thomas was driving, and even so in the car Astrid had felt drunk. It was after midnight when Thomas drew up outside her apartment and then simply went up with her. The tension between them was so great there was no other possibility than touching, than holding on to each other. Everything else had happened perfectly naturally. Really? said Thomas. Do you always come as quickly as that? Astrid smiled and shrugged. She didn't feel like talking, and without turning a light on went into the kitchen for a glass of water. Thomas followed her. As she stood by the sink, he put his arms around her from behind and she felt that he was still aroused. Hurry, he said. She turned, took a sip of water, with her arms crossed in front of her, then passed him the glass. He set it down on the counter, took her hand, and led her back to the bedroom. That was the enduring image Astrid had of their first night together: walking through the apartment hand in hand, and naked.

Later on, Thomas told her that he had loved her from the very beginning, was eaten up with desire for her. He told her without pathos, more with the pride of a successful long-distance runner, describing the torments of a recently finished marathon. From his tone, Astrid could tell he was also interested to hear whether that had been the case with her as well, if she had been in love with him in the same way, dreaming of him, sending him hidden signals. She was so tired she kept drifting away, and sometimes couldn't be sure whether she had been sleeping or had heard Thomas speaking or just dreamed of it. You still there? he asked. Yes, she said. Nothing more. She listened to him describing their first meeting in the bookstore, a masked ball in the *Traube*, going to a concert with her and her boyfriend in the city. She remembered the occasions, but Thomas's version was so different from her own, a story full of love and despair and hope, in which every word, every facial expression, every gesture had its significance. Had she not noticed anything then? No, she would have had to say. I liked you, but I wasn't in love with you and I didn't feel your love either. So why did she take him up to her apartment that time? Not everything you did had a reason. It was no big thing, more a sequence of small decisions, aimless in themselves, part negligence, part giving in. Not to take her hand back when he took it in his, not to turn her head away when he tried to kiss her, to stay sitting in the car until he turned off the ignition, not to say anything when he got out with you, went up the stairs behind you, walked into your apartment with you. I could never picture you in a sexual situation, said Thomas, with his head in her lap. I don't know why, I just couldn't. I couldn't even picture you naked. She didn't know whether his words were a compliment or just a simple statement of fact, and whether he expected an answer from her and if so what. It had never even occurred to her to picture Thomas naked or in a sexual situation. Not that she was someone who pictured things to herself anyway, she didn't plan ahead or obsessively rehash the past. When Thomas talked about their relationship, even later on, when they'd been together for a long time, she was always surprised how complicated everything was in his head. But she liked the stories, and the feeling that their history was deep and complicated and inevitable. You're so beautiful when you come, he said. Your smile, your movements. He wouldn't stop talking. Are you still there? Yes. I love you. I need to sleep now, said Astrid. Your arms, he went on, you have beautiful arms, your shoulders, your back, the lovely dimples over your bottom. Is that right, said Astrid. She switched on the light to set the alarm, then turned it off, and rolled away from Thomas. In the darkness she could feel his hands, his warm body, his kisses. They made love again, more vehemently than before, like a silent tussle, as though they couldn't get close enough to each other. Astrid no longer felt her body as a whole, only in parts, in Thomas's touch, his weight, the force with which he held down her hands over her head.

She lay in the dark, with a smile on her face at the thought of that first night with Thomas. The mixture of tenderness and force with which he explored and took her. It had still taken quite some time after that before they became a couple.

Thomas got up early and packed his rucksack. He didn't have many more possessions than two months ago, when he moved in. The widow was already up and about, reading the local paper in the kitchen. Thomas said he needed to be moving on. She made difficulties, said he should have told her sooner, she couldn't find another tenant at the drop of a hat. She looked reproachfully at him. He suggested paying half of next week's rent, and she finally accepted his offer, though not without complaining again about the difficulties he was creating by suddenly moving out. In the end, she offered him coffee—perhaps she hoped to hear why he was going. He declined, paid her, and left.

The carpenter wasn't pleased about his leaving either. He praised Thomas's work and application and even offered him a raise. What will you be going on to? he asked, once he'd accepted that he couldn't change Thomas's mind. I need to be moving on, said Thomas.

The distance that took less than fifteen minutes in the carpenter's car took him more than two hours on foot. The footpath was covered in snow, so he was obliged to walk along the highway, which switchbacked up the narrow coulee and kept plunging into galleries and tunnels. In some places there was no sidewalk, and Thomas was forced to press himself against the side of the tunnel as a hooting tourist bus swept past him. Shortly after Thomas had emerged from the last gallery, and the upland valley opened out in front of him, a police patrol car drew up alongside him. The officer in the front passenger seat wound down the window and asked if everything was all right. Not exactly hiking weather, he said, and asked to see his ID. He gave it a cursory look and wished him a nice day.

For the rest of the winter, Thomas was employed as kitchen assistant in a restaurant where he was also given accommodations. The chef, an Israeli man who had married the daughter of the owner and later took over the business, paid him accordingly, though he upped his wages as Thomas took on more demanding tasks from week to week. You might have made a chef, you know, said David. Sometimes Thomas could feel himself under observation, but his boss's motivation seemed to be less curiosity than simple liking. Then David told him about his early time in this area, how difficult it was to establish himself and get used to the people, the landscape, and the weather. He and his wife had two boys, a seven-year-old and a five-year-old, who often hung around the kitchens or the restaurant. Then it was Thomas's turn to watch David and marvel at his tender, almost motherly way with the boys.

By the time the ski season wound down in April and the number of visitors declined, Thomas had managed to put away a bit of money. David asked him what his plans were. Thomas said he thought he would cross the Gotthard Pass and continue south.

The highway service had been working on removing snow for several weeks now, but the pass wouldn't be open until Pentecost at the earliest. Thomas spent a couple of rainy days waiting, for the most part in his room. The day it brightened up, he set off. David had prepared an elaborate lunch, and he and his wife and even the boys had embraced him outside the restaurant when he left, quite as though he were family.

Shortly before the turnoff to the pass there was a little wayside chapel. Here is the parting of the ways, friend, which way will you take? it said over the entrance. Do you want to go to the Eternal City? Down to Holy Colonia on the German Rhine, or westward to the Franks? After months in one place, Thomas felt the high of being on the road again, the anticipation of a future that was not prescribed and that could, with every step, be altered.

The pastures in the valley were green already, but not far above the village the pass road was barred. The higher he climbed, the more snow he came upon, first only in hollows and on the shady side of valleys, but farther up it was an unbroken sheet. While it had been raining for the past few days in the valley, up here the road that had been cleared was snowed shut again. A little way before the head of the pass, Thomas encountered workmen who were just eating lunch in the sun, beside great gouged-out piles of snow. He asked them about the state of the path, and they warned him about one spot where a retaining board had worked loose, that wasn't yet shored up. They seemed unsurprised to see a hiker. Maybe there were a lot like himself, thought Thomas, maybe he was one element of a brotherhood of wanderers spread over the five continents. He thought about the migrations of animals, the movements of birds and fish from continent to continent, movement all over the world. It struck him as a more natural mode of being than settlement in one place.

The road ran along between walls of snow that were several yards high. On the slopes he kept seeing the traces of avalanches, in some places the hard icy chunks had almost made it down as far as the road.

At the head of the pass a strong cold wind was blowing. The sky was a deep blue, and Thomas could feel the burning warmth of the sun in his face. He spread out his coat on the snow and sat down to eat. He was looking south, the view ringed by a blaze of light.

By now, Astrid had to reckon up the time when someone asked her how long it was that Thomas had been dead. He went away two years ago, she would say, or three years, or six years. But she still wore her wedding ring, the phone book contained both their names, and when she was called upon to define her legal status, she would always check married. Each time, without asking, the tax official would change her entry to widowed, a word that Astrid could no more get used to than fatherless for the children.

Konrad had done the legally required minimum time at school and landed a traineeship at an insurance firm. In the summer he wanted to temp, to save up for a motor scooter.

He had recently started asking about his father. Then Astrid would tell him this or that, but each time she felt painfully aware how little she knew about Thomas, and how little what she did know was able to convey about him. Each story was a betrayal of him, each account a tacit decision, this is the way it was, this is how it would always be remembered. Or perhaps it wasn't like that at all, she said. She said, You take after him, and that seemed to make Konrad happy.

Ella had passed her leaving exam and was going on to college to study Romance languages. She would have loved to go to France for a month or two to brush up on her French. She had written for information from various language schools, and showed her mother the glossy brochures, where cheerful young people were shown sitting in classrooms, or riding on horseback, or on surfboards. Astrid just looked at the prices. We can't afford that, she said, why don't you try and get a job as an au pair? After Thomas's disappearance, she'd had to tighten their belts, in spite of the pension. In the early years she was often asked by friends whether she didn't want to go back to work. There was a job going here, or someone was looking for a person to help out in the office. When her onetime boss gave up the bookstore for reasons of age, she asked Astrid if she had any interest in taking it over. But even after the children had gotten older and more independent, she wasn't interested in working. She didn't apply anywhere. It wasn't that she was depressed, as Manuela supposed when she came to mind the children for a day or two from time to time, so that Astrid could go away somewhere. Perhaps it's just that I don't want anything to change, she said. That would be tantamount to acknowledging that your husband is dead, said Patrick. Stop playing the amateur psychologist, said Astrid, I liked you better when you were a policeman. Anyway, you don't want anything to change either. Then we're agreed, said Patrick.

Later they went for a walk along the lakefront, talking about their children like two old friends. It's no bad thing if Ella appreciates that we can't afford everything, said Astrid. We're not badly off. I can understand her disappointment, said Patrick. At her age, you just want to blend in. But that doesn't excuse her language, said Astrid. Ella had called her father an asshole. Just because that asshole dumped us, she said, now I can't go to language school. Then she had run off upstairs and locked herself in her room. Astrid had canceled her pocket money for the next month. You can be terribly hard sometimes, you know, said Patrick. Basically Ella's right, even if she should have said it some other way. Now don't you start too, said Astrid, and walked faster, as though to run away from him, or the things he was saying. Patrick sped up too. You won't hear a word against him, he said, admit that he behaved like a son of a bitch. Astrid made no reply.

Eventually the contact with Patrick came to an end; there wasn't any particular time or reason, Astrid didn't even know which of them had stopped calling. She bought herself a dog.

The weeks passed, and the months and years. Konrad completed his traineeship and moved to the city. Ella went to Lyon to do a second degree. This was the time when Astrid sometimes wondered if it wouldn't have been better if she'd never met Thomas and had married someone else who would still be around. But she rejected that thought after a while; it wasn't possible to take Thomas out of her life like an object that had lost its utility, he was a part of her, just as she was a part of him, no matter what had happened and would happen.

Ella came back from Lyon pregnant by a man she didn't want to live with. She took a job as a schoolteacher. After not being in touch with Astrid for a long time, she was glad now that she was there to mind the baby. Emilie spent two days a week with her grandmother, then when she started kindergarten, just two afternoons. Konrad married a woman who was seven years older than him and didn't want children. They went on an around-the-world tour that must have cost a fortune. He always used to call his mother every week. Before he set off, he fixed her up with a Skype account, but after a couple of times, Astrid asked him to go back to standard phoning, he felt closer to her that way. How are you? You all right? he asked. Yes, she said. I'm fine.

The years had no particular chronology, the journeys no direction, the places stood in no discernible relation to one another. Thomas took on casual work that got him through the times when he earned nothing or rested or moved on. In Italy he worked off the books until he was caught and had to go; in France he got a new set of papers from people he would sooner have had nothing to do with. He worked as a janitor in a discount mall in the middle of nowhere, then as a janitor in an autobahn rest stop. When he had enough of the countryside, he went to Lyon and delivered bread for a large bakery. He had to get up extremely early, but it meant he got the afternoons off. Once he was involved in a minor accident, nothing grave, but the police ascertained that he had no driver's license, and he was out of a job. For a time then he didn't work at all, drank too much, and lived in ever shittier rooms. Then he got a grip, first helped out in a homeless kitchen, and got another job in a restaurant. He spent a year on the Irish island the teacher had shown him photographs of, at any rate he was pretty sure it was the same place. He had never forgotten those pictures of the landscape, the cliffs, the black-faced sheep, the endless sea that made him feel nostalgic and secure at the same time, only the name of the island, like that of the teacher, had slipped his mind. When there was no more work, he returned to the Continent, first to France again, then Germany. He had occasional affairs with women who tended to be just as lost as he was. At brief moments of arousal he sometimes managed not to think of Astrid. But as soon as the women were gone, he would think of her again, and he would feel ashamed of himself for his infidelity and clear off. He got along with almost everyone he worked with but felt no desire to be closer to any of them. Best of all he got along with children, because he could tell them anything. The thought that his own were by now grown up felt strange to him; he didn't feel anything for their maturity, on the contrary it was as though they had taken something from him. When he thought of them, it was always the way they were when he had left. He remembered the last vacation they had all taken together, and he remembered the feeling that had kept sneaking up on him then, that he could never get close enough to them, that they were inevitably distancing themselves from him, as though following a law of nature.

For a couple of years he had a dog, a stray like himself, who had followed him and whom he kept with him, even though it made for a lot of difficulties. One night his dog died after not eating for several days. Thomas buried him in the bushes at the side of the road. This was in Greece somewhere. That was the farthest away he got; he didn't want to leave Europe, the rest of the world felt somehow too remote to him, and too far from home.

In his choice of places, he followed his instincts. Sometimes he went south, then north, sometimes closer to home, sometimes farther away. In all those years he never crossed into Switzerland, but it wasn't a decision as such, it just happened that way. Not everything you did had a reason.

It was the end of May, two months after Thomas's birthday; he had now reached retirement age, though in his false passport he was two years younger. When the forgers had asked him for his date of birth, he had given them Astrid's— he had no idea why.

He had spent that winter in Spain, minding a holiday home north of Barcelona that belonged to one of his previous employers. Two weeks ago, he had gone into the city and hopped on a bus, the first one going, and that had taken him to Freiburg im Breisgau. Although he had a bad back and could no longer lift heavy weights, he needed money after the months of idleness in Spain and took a job as a housepainter, as there was nothing else going just then.

It was a cold, rainy day. Thomas stood up on the scaffolding, painting under the eaves of a single-family home. Below him, the others were applying an undercoat to the front. Thomas heard a car draw up. In turning to see who it was, he took a step back and knocked against the bucket, sending some of the paint splattering onto the asphalt below. The boss had climbed out of the truck, looked up, and called out, You fucking idiot, can't you watch what you're doing. Thomas draped himself over the rail, and the cold and rain and the gray asphalt and the green of the grass took him back twenty years to the edge of the grike he had fallen into. A wind splashed a few raindrops into his face, and while his boss was still effing and blinding down below, his voice seemed to be getting quieter, and Thomas had the feeling that the rain was letting up, and there was a break in the clouds, and he was falling into a sky full of dazzling light.

Astrid stood in the kitchen, washing up from lunch. The day before, Ella and Emilie had been to visit, and Astrid had baked a cake because it was Emilie's first day at school. She had given Ella what was left of the cake, and at her insistence kept a little piece for herself. She took the cling wrap off the plate and set it down on the kitchen table. The window was open over the sink, all around it was peaceful, just a blackbird was breaking the silence with its irritated twitter. Astrid went outside to put the vegetable peelings into the compost. She shooed away the cat that was slinking about around the plum tree. Back inside, she put on water for coffee, tipped some grounds into the filter, and stood there to watch small and larger bubbles forming in the water. Her dog, an old Labrador, came trotting into the kitchen and sniffed at its empty dish. Astrid saw him lift his head and prick up his ears even before she had consciously taken in the squeak of the unoiled gate. Then she knew he was back. She gave no thought to the hurt and the offense, or to what had been and what might be. She ran into the living room and through the window caught sight not so much of the man as of his movements, his typical walk, slightly leaning forward, slightly stiff, but swift and resolute. She heard his footsteps on the gravel, then they stopped, and Astrid had the sensation that her heart had stopped with them. He might still turn back and disappear forever. But he was only hesitating or perhaps savoring the moment. With a bewildered smile he looked around at the blooming garden, taking stock of the changes, marveling at the huge rhubarb patch, the plum tree that twenty years ago when he left had been a little sapling. He noticed that the elder bush was gone, that the wire-mesh fence had been removed and the adjacent gardens had been allowed to grow together, as though they belonged together, that new people had moved in next door, who had left their own traces too, a swing set and a small wooden sandbox, the tricycle by the door and the ball on the lawn. His stopping felt unendingly long to Astrid, in the complete silence she could hear the rushing of the blood in her ears. Then there were his footsteps again, labored, as though he found it difficult to go up the stairs. And suddenly Astrid felt perfectly convinced that in all those years Thomas had led no other life, that he'd had no other relationship, not fathered any children, not even practiced his profession, further qualified himself or grown in any way. Just like her he had been awaiting this moment, this brief moment of happiness in which he would put out his hand and turn the doorknob. This moment of the door opening, when she would see his indistinct form in the dazzling noonday light.

PETER STAMM is the author of the novels *Agnes, All Days Are Night, Seven Years, On a Day Like This,* and *Unformed Landscape,* and the short-story collections *We're Flying* and *In Strange Gardens and Other Stories.* His prize-winning books have been translated into more than thirty languages. For his entire body of work and his accomplishments in fiction, he was short-listed for the Man Booker International Prize in 2013, and in 2014 he won the prestigious Friedrich Hölderlin Prize. He lives in Switzerland.

MICHAEL HOFMANN has translated the work of Gottfried Benn, Hans Fallada, Franz Kafka, Joseph Roth, and many others. In 2012 he was awarded the Thornton Wilder Prize for Translation by the American Academy of Arts and Letters. His *Selected Poems* was published in 2009, and *Where Have You Been? Selected Essays* in 2014. He lives in Florida and London.

Keep in touch with
Granta Books:

Visit grantabooks.com to discover more.

GRANTA

Also available from Granta Books
www.grantabooks.com

WE'RE FLYING

Peter Stamm

Translated by Michael Hofmann

SHORTLISTED FOR THE FRANK O'CONNOR INTERNATIONAL SHORT STORY AWARD

'An extraordinary author who can make the ordinary absolutely electrifying . . . Hard to recommend too highly' *The Times*, 'Books of the Year'

In this astute, beautifully composed collection, a woman becomes involved with her younger upstairs neighbour; a man waits for the outcome of medical tests; and a young couple learns to navigate the thrills and complications of cohabitation. A master of the short story, Stamm does not spare the reader's feelings, nor does he waste a word.

'There is something extraordinary in Stamm's ability to make normal situations, described in such minimalist prose, so engrossing and affecting . . . Hofmann's translation is precise and irresistibly readable' *Prospect*

'Original, assured and utterly beguiling' *Daily Mail*

'One of Europe's most exciting writers . . . a writer to read, and read often' *New York Times*

'Stamm cuts through the surface of things . . . Each story is intriguing like a complex piece of machinery where you can see everything even if you don't understand how it works' Tessa Hadley, author of *Married Love*

'A pleasure to read'
Independent

All DAYS ARE NIGHT

Peter Stamm

Translated by Michael Hofmann

'A brilliant, bruising tale of shattered lives' *Independent*

Gillian seems to have it all – she is beautiful, successful, and securely married. But one night after an argument with her husband, their car crashes on a wet road. When Gillian wakes in the hospital, she is a widow with a ruined face who must now revisit the past in order to make sense of her altered existence and begin to glimpse the freedom that might come with her loss.

'Everything Peter Stamm turns his hand to is highly disturbing, acutely perceptive, and unfathomably gripping, and *All Days Are Night* is no exception. In sentences that are plain and surgical, in prose that has about it a disquieting stillness, he dissects our fractured lives. A masterpiece of disorientation and control, *All Days Are Night* may be his best novel yet' Rupert Thomson, author of *Secrecy*

'Stamm's prose, in a crystalline translation by Michael Hofmann, is as sharply illuminating as a surgical light. A profound and mysterious novel about life, love and hiding – from a master writer' *Economist*

'*All Days Are Night* recuperates one of the biggest themes any novelist can tackle with austere, formal brilliance' *Financial Times*

'Magnificent . . . as fascinating as the studies of any anthropologist' *Guardian*

'A small gem about starting over when you have nothing left' ★★★★ *Metro*

Also available from Granta Books
www.grantabooks.com

SEVEN YEARS

Peter Stamm

Translated by Michael Hofmann

'*Seven Years* is a novel to make you doubt your own dogma.
What more can a novel do than that?' Zadie Smith

Alex is caught between two very different women. Sonia, his
wife, is intelligent, beautiful, charming, and ambitious. Together
they have established a prestigious architecture firm and a life
of luxury. But long hours and failed attempts at starting a family
bring about the seven-year itch, and soon Alex begins an affair
with dull, passive Ivona, with devastating consequences.

'How many writers have written with this degree of brutal
perceptiveness and wisdom about the indeterminate depths of
heterosexual desire? Wharton, Roth (sometimes), James Salter,
Kundera. Stamm inscribes his name on that august list. Quietly
shattering' *The Times*

'I love this novel . . . It has the makings of an existential classic'
Sunday Telegraph

'Cool and immensely accomplished' Adam Mars-Jones, *Observer*

'Quietly spectacular' *New Yorker*

'Mesmeric . . . the ripples that it sets in motion radiate in the
reader's mind long after the novel's conversation has ended' *TLS*

'Cool, incisively told and deeply, unsettlingly strange, *Seven Years*
held me, gripped me' Julie Myerson